BLOOD ON MEGIDDO

AN ALEX MASON THRILLER

DAVID ARCHER

BLAKE BANNER

RIGHTHOUSE

PRAISE FOR ALEX MASON

ALEX MASON THRILLERS
Odin (Book 1)
Ice Cold Spy (Book 2)
Mason's Law (Book 3)
Assets and Liabilities (Book 4)
Russian Roulette (Book 5)
Executive Order (Book 6)
Dead Man Talking (Book 7)
All The King's Men (Book 8)
Flashpoint (Book 9)
Brotherhood of the Goat (Book 10)
Dead Hot (Book 11)
Blood on Megiddo (Book 12)
Son of Hell (Book 13)

PROLOGUE

David dropped into his red faux leather chair and rattled at the keys of his computer. The room was dark, and the light from the screen lay across the planes of his face. Miriam's voice came to him from down the hall in the living room.

"*Ten minutes!*"

He saw the deposit in his account and smiled. Twenty grand. The fifth such deposit in as many months. He felt mildly conflicted. He knew he should feel guilty. He was betraying his wife and his country, but he was enjoying the rewards far too much to feel anything but the thrill and the excitement of the game.

He knew that people would die. But he had no doubt in his mind that those people would die anyway. Ben had said as much. God had taken Israel as his chosen land, and in so doing, he had made it the land of war and the home of the dispossessed. Because those who followed Elohim, Yahweh, Allah, whether they were Jews, Christians or Muslims, followed him as warriors. For He was truly the God of War. From his banishment of Adam and Eve from the Garden— before that even! From the moment He forbad the consuming of the fruit of the Tree of Knowledge—He declared himself the father of conflict and war.

So all those who followed Him, those who lived by the sword of God, must surely die by that sword. Surely, he told himself, gazing at the one hundred thousand dollars sitting in his account in Panama, the history of the three Abrahamic religions spawned by this so-called God of Love and Forgiveness showed that he was indeed a deity of blood and violence and vengeance.

"*You coming or do I have to eat alone?*"

"*I'm coming!*"

He went to stand but paused. A red dot on his taskbar told him he had a message. He opened it and saw it was from his contact. He had never met his contact. He knew him only as Ben. Ben had told him that the whole idea of the dead drop belonged to last century. Dead drops were now electronic, and all the information David sold him he sent electronically using an encoding device connected to a highly sophisticated VPN. So it was impossible for anyone but Ben to know what information was encoded into the message or where it came from. That was the way Ben had described it.

He opened the message. It read simply: *I need to see you in person*

He sat staring at it, blinking occasionally but other than that immobile. He had no frame of reference upon which to base a response.

"*I'm taking the pizzas out of the oven! Are you coming or not?*"

He gave a small start. Then, over his shoulder, "*Yeah! Yes! On my way!*"

He typed out rapidly, *That is against protocol.*

You do not instruct me in protocol. You do as I say. I pay you.

He hesitated. *Where and when?*

"*David! What are you doing? Come on!*"

He waited. He heard the oven door close with an irritated slam. Then the television, louder than necessary.

I'll contact you soon

His hands reached for the keyboard. He needed more information, more assurances, but another message appeared: *It is time for your pizza. Go. Do not raise suspicion.*

He went cold. An icy shudder moved through his skin. He stood, backed a couple of steps away from the computer, and hurried down the passage to the living room, where Miriam was watching the TV. She didn't look up or acknowledge him as he came in. His pizza was on the long coffee table between the sofa and the TV, where they ate every night.

"Sorry, babe. I had a message. Work."

She gave her head a small shake. "'S'all right. I'm getting used to it."

He dropped next to her on the sofa and tried to nuzzle her ear. "Come on, babe. It's work. You know that."

She pulled away. "I'm trying to hear the news. Bloody Yanks! Allies when it suits them, but don't put the flow of oil at risk!"

He sighed and reached for his pizza. The TV was saying, "Mr. Netanyahu made an impassioned speech in which he pointed to the fact that the last ceasefire in which hostages were supposed to be released by Hamas led to the ruthless execution of six of those hostages and a barrage of rockets being directed at Israeli residential suburbs and increased attacks from Hezbollah and Houthi pirates..."

"Ceasefire!" She spat the words. "They know that every ceasefire is a chance for them to regroup and rearm."

He was about to answer when his phone pinged. He pulled it from his back pocket and saw it was a message from Ben.

Go downstairs and open the door

He hesitated. She sensed it and looked at him. "What?"

"I..." He struggled for a second to think of an explanation that made sense.

"*What?*"

He shrugged and grinned. "I have to go downstairs for a moment."

"What the hell, David?"

"It's work. I won't be a moment. I'll be right back."

He swung over the back of the sofa, crossed the living room, and stepped out onto the landing. It was just one story, and he skipped down the stairs three at a time. It was faster than waiting for the ancient elevator.

The main doors of the apartment block were dark, wood-and-brass frames with large panels of glass. Through them, as he crossed the lobby, he could see only blackness stained with wet smudges of amber light. He pushed the right door open and stood with his foot wedged against it, looking up and down Gloucester Terrace. He didn't see anything but wet cars parked under the tall streetlamps in the eternal London drizzle.

There was no traffic, but across the road, thirty or forty

yards to his right, a car inched away from the sidewalk. He frowned because the headlamps remained off, and the way the light from the streetlamps above hit the glass, it seemed there was no driver behind the wheel. He knew there were driverless cabs now, but they were in sunshine cities like San Francisco and Phoenix, not New York or London.

He watched it as it approached in electronic silence. When it was directly opposite him, it slowed to a halt. He wondered for a second if he was intended to get in, but he didn't wonder for long.

The broad-headed dart that struck his chest was projected using compressed air. It was traveling at seventy feet per second with a force of no more than forty-five joules, but it was razor sharp and sliced clean through his fifth intercostal and his heart and exited his back to land on the sage green carpet of the lobby behind him.

The hemorrhage from his heart was massive, and he had faded into death in no more than a second, before he'd hit the sidewalk. The electric vehicle moved silently into the night, and David fell forward like a felled tree onto the short walkway that lead to the sidewalk.

Upstairs in his den, his computer had been switched on remotely. All the files, apps, and programs were systematically and very rapidly deleted, as was the entire operating system. Simultaneously, the Kensington Police Station on Earls Court Road was being notified that a homicide had been committed outside 101 Gloucester Terrace.

Shortly after that, the wail of sirens howled under the low, orange ceiling of cloud, but Miriam, watching the news just thirty feet above her dead husband, did not hear them.

ONE

IT WAS RAINING. SOMETIMES IT SEEMED THAT IN London it was always raining. There are places in the world, like India or Brunei, where the rain can look silver, or even at times gold, but in London, the rain seems always to be gray. It looked especially gray on that November morning, Thursday the 9th, as we stood under a large beach umbrella brightly decorated in primary colors and watched a small group gathered around a grave some thirty feet away, where David Jones was about to be lowered six feet into the ground. The rabbi had said a few prayers, and now the congregation were reciting the Mourner's Kaddish.

"Do you see anyone of interest?"

Gallin shook her head. "A couple of guys from GCHQ, but you'd expect them to be here. The rest are family."

"The woman picking up the spade, that's Miriam?"

"Yup."

"She has the spade the wrong way around."

"It's a tradition."

"Right."

I was thinking about how illogical things, like smashing plates and glasses and using the wrong side of a spade, could become logical by calling it a tradition, when the congregation began to break up. They all took turns hugging Miriam and then dispersed in search of their cars. Gallin gave voice to my thoughts.

"Apparently nobody's taking Miriam home. That's interesting."

I made a noise of thoughtful agreement and watched as Miriam turned away from the grave and made her way toward us. She looked drawn and gray, like the rain, like the day in general.

She stopped some six feet away with her veil raised onto her pillbox hat and a black umbrella over her head.

"Who are you?"

"My name is Alex Mason. This is Aila Gallin. We were colleagues of your husband."

She glanced at us both, back and forth. "Mason and Gallin, you're Jewish?"

Gallin answered for us, "I am. We realize this must be a very painful time for you. But you understand we need to talk to you."

"Can I see some ID?"

Gallin showed her her card, and I showed her one that said I worked for the Pentagon. "We may as well get it over with. You can come back to our apartment"—a small flinch —"to my apartment."

I glanced around. "You have a car?"

She shook her head. "My brother-in-law brought me. I told him I wanted to walk home."

"You want to ride with us? We'll keep it as brief as possible."

"Fine. I assume you know the way."

It was a ten-minute drive, and all the way she was silent, sitting in the back seat of Gallin's old S-Type Jag, watching the endless terraces of Victorian houses slip by. We eventually pulled up across from her house. She climbed out and crossed the road to her apartment block without saying anything, while we climbed out, locked the car, and followed after her at a trot through the drizzle.

Upstairs, she left her front door open for us and pushed through to the kitchen, taking off her coat as she went. The living room was roughly square, large by London standards because it dated from the '20s or the '30s, when there was still space for human beings in the city. They had a sofa in the middle of the room, set to face the TV, and a coffee table placed so you could eat off it while receiving your daily dose of remote conditioning. On the table was a pizza carton and a can of Coke. A table in the bay window over on the right looked like it didn't get much use.

Her voice came from the kitchen.

"You want tea? I need a cup."

I let Gallin answer that we didn't. "We don't want to take up a lot of your time, Miriam."

She came out a moment later with a steaming mug and sat on the sofa. Gallin sat beside her with her back against the arm, and I brought over a chair from the table. I leaned forward, with my elbows on my knees.

"Miriam, I know this is going to be hard, so you take whatever time you need, but you're in the trade, and you know we have to go through this, right?"

She nodded at her mug of tea, which she held cupped in both hands.

"We need you to tell us exactly what happened that night, and anything that might stand out as strange or unusual. Start wherever you like, include anything you feel might be relevant."

The first thing she said was, "We are both Jewish. We were both originally attached to the Five Eyes intelligence sharing program. As you know, since the Second World War, the Five Eyes have been the five principal English speaking democracies, but since nine-eleven, with the rise of Islamic terrorism, Israel has increasingly been read into Five Eyes briefings. Since 1999, English is no longer an official language in Israel, but in practice, it retains a role which is comparable to an official language, and pretty much everyone speaks English. In terms of Israel's military and intelligence relationship with the United States and the United Kingdom, English is fundamental."

She paused, and we waited in silence. She sipped her tea and sighed.

"A few years ago, the Five Eyes decided to establish a protocol by which Israel became a kind of associate member with a dedicated department. Not only was it vital in order to protect Israel against Hamas and Hezbollah, but the Mossad had become an invaluable, even essential, source of intelligence on Islamic terrorist threats. Because of our Jewish backgrounds, David and I were assigned to that department."

Gallin said gently, "That much we know, Miriam."

Miriam spoke, staring into her mug of tea. "You said I

could tell you in my own way and in my own time. Let me gather my thoughts."

Her tone was resentful, strained. Gallin nodded. "Sure."

"I guess it was about five or six months ago, I started noticing something a bit odd in Dave's behavior. I didn't really pay much attention at first. Our business is all about privacy and discretion, right? So you don't pry into what is going on in other people's lives unless you want trouble."

I said, "What was odd about his behavior, Miriam? What were the things you noticed?"

She puffed her cheeks, and her gaze became abstracted, like she was looking at something neither Gallin nor I could see, some memory, some absent scene.

"It's hard to put your finger on. Sometimes he didn't seem to be present." Her gaze returned, and she frowned at me. "You know what I mean? We'd be sitting in the pub or having dinner, and he'd seem not to be there. Then sometimes, when we were out, he'd get up to go to the loo, but when he came back, he came from the street instead of the loos."

Gallin said, "So he'd been outside?"

Miriam nodded. I asked, "You think he'd been making a call or receiving one?"

She nodded again. "Or seeing someone. That was the impression." She hitched her shoulders a fraction of an inch. "But that's the work we do. So I pretended not to notice. The thing is, it got more and more, and he started spending long periods of time in his study on his computer. A couple of times I went in and he immediately closed whatever he was doing. The second time he did it, I challenged him about it. Frankly, I was beginning to wonder whether he was having an affair. He told me it was work and I should not ask him about it."

"And what happened the day before yesterday? Take your time."

She was quiet for a moment, looking over at the window. The rain had grown heavier and occasionally lashed a rapid tattoo on the glass.

"We had come home together early, about four o'clock. We had managed to wangle a long weekend together, Thursday evening and then Friday through to Monday morning. It was a luxury, and we were looking forward to it.

"I guess it was about six o'clock. I'd put a couple of pizzas in the oven, and we were going to watch a movie together." She smiled a private smile. "It was an old one we both loved. Ustinov, James Mason, Maggie Smith and Diana Rigg. *Evil under the Sun*."

As she said the title, her smile faded.

"While the pizzas were in the oven, he went to his study. I got cross and started calling him. He did what he always did: 'Yeah, yeah, I'm on my way.' So I switched on the news. To be honest, he didn't actually take that long, but I was so sick of his weird behavior and the feeling I was being cut out that I just ignored him."

She stopped and sat staring at the floor.

"What happened then, Miriam?"

"He received a Whatsapp." She said it to the floor.

Gallin asked, "Who from?"

"I don't know. He said he had to go downstairs. I was just so..." She shook her head and took a deep breath. When she started talking again, she was weeping. "I was so sick of his stupid behavior. I just ignored him. And that was the last time I ever saw him. The last time we ever spoke to each other."

"Did he say anything, anything at all about the message?"

She pulled a handkerchief from her sleeve, mopped her eyes, and blew her nose.

"I asked him what it was. He said he had to go downstairs. I said something like, 'What the hell?' and he told me it was work. He went downstairs, and after a while, I heard the sirens outside the window. By that time, he was dead."

We were quiet for a moment. The wind had picked up outside. The rain was tapping at the glass in a broken rhythm, and a damp cold crept into my ankles and the back of my neck. Eventually Gallin asked, "Your office contacted you, right?"

"Yes."

"They told you not to touch any of his possessions and to hand them over to us if we wanted them."

Miriam gave a single nod. "His phone and his computer are in his office. I looked for his last Whatsapp message. I know I wasn't supposed to, but I had to."

I asked, "Who was it from?"

She turned her head and looked at me with exhausted, wet eyes. "Everything on his phone has been wiped. There is nothing."

Gallin scowled. "*Everything?*"

Miriam wiped her eyes on the back of her cuff. "There is no software—zero software—on Dave's phone. I haven't touched his computer. So your guess is as good as mine. It's all yours."

"You mind if we have a look?"

I asked out of courtesy; we all three knew she couldn't say no.

"Like I said, it's all yours."

Gallin stood, and I followed her down to David's small office. She pulled on some latex gloves and took a small black box from her jacket pocket. She connected it to the USB port and switched on the PC. If there was a password, the decoder would crack it in thirty seconds or less.

There wasn't a password. There might have been once, but right then, there was nothing, not even an operating system. Like the phone, the computer had no software at all. Gallin looked up at me. Besides a small twitch between her eyebrows, there was no expression on her face. I turned and walked back to the living room.

"Has anyone been into your apartment since David's death?"

She shook her head. "No, nobody."

"Nobody has touched his computer."

"No."

"We'll need to take it away with us."

She shrugged. "It's not mine. It wasn't even his. It belongs to the government."

Gallin emerged from the study behind me carrying a leather case. In her right hand she had her cell held to her ear.

"I'm bringing his laptop and a couple of external drives, but you'd better send in forensics. His computer and his cell were both wiped clean..." She shook her head like whoever she was talking to could see her. "No," she said, "I mean wiped *clean*. There isn't even an operating system. You need to go over this place with an electron microscope, and you need to take Miriam somewhere safe."

Miriam closed her eyes and sank back into her chair.

TWO

We were at Whitehall Court, just beside Whitehall Gardens on the River Thames. Sir Lacklan Orme, who had arrived on his bicycle while we were parking Gallin's Jag, sat behind his vast oak desk, which, he claimed, had graffiti carved into it dating back to the fifteenth century.

Sir Lacklan was smaller than his desk, but about as old. He had wispy white hair that had once been blond and still clung to that memory. He had a Savile Row suit carefully tailored not to look too elegant and eyes that were as sharp as razor blades fresh out of the pack.

Gallin was standing at the window, looking down at the park and the river.

"I've just been talking to your father," he told her.

Her father, whom she sometimes referred to as Gabriel, was the head of the Mossad's unofficial mission in London.

"We agreed these are very worrying times. It reminds me of the early thirties, when fascism was brewing all over

Europe but nobody could see it. Nobody believed it, except Winston, of course. He kept trying to warn everyone, but they just laughed at him and called him a warmonger."

Gallin turned to face him, and the window behind her cast her face into deep shadow. "And look what happened then," she said.

"Quite so. Historically, you know, peace in Europe—peace in the West, indeed, is a terribly recent thing, and very fragile." He smiled. "Post-war generations tend to think of it as the norm, but it isn't, not by a long shot."

Gallin said, "In Israel, we don't think of it as the norm."

"No, you wouldn't." His face became abstracted. "War follows you, doesn't it? You are the children of the God of War, it seems."

"There is no god," she answered, "only war."

His face produced a small wince, and he looked down at the file before him on his desk.

"David Jones was shot with a dart," he said. "It was carbon steel and razor sharp. It had no scorching. It had not been subjected to intense heat, so it was either shot from a crossbow or, more likely, judging from its design, it was shot from some kind of compressed air device."

I asked, "No witnesses?"

"None. It was dinner time on a rainy, cold evening. There was no one on the street and no one looking out of the window. All we can piece together is that he received some kind of message on his mobile phone that instructed him to go downstairs. Once there, he was shot with that dart which all but severed his heart in two."

Gallin said, "And just moments before that, he had been on his computer. But ten minutes after he was killed, his cell was wiped clean, even of its operating system, and some time between then and this morning, the same thing happened to his computer."

"Correct, and as of this moment, we have absolutely no idea how that was achieved or why he was killed."

I drummed a little tattoo on the arm of my chair. "He had been receiving text messages and emails which he told Miriam had to do with work, and he couldn't tell her about them."

He frowned at me. "Really? I mean—" He spread his hands and gave a little sigh. "Strictly speaking, that is true of all our officers. Whether they are married to each other—something we discourage, naturally—or merely friends or acquaintances. They should never discuss work outside of the office, so to speak. But in David's case, he was employed in intelligence analysis relating to Israel, Lebanon, Syria, Jordan, Egypt, Hamas and Hezbollah, Houthi, naturally, and of course Iran. That, in general terms, was his work." He raised his eyebrows high and gave his head a small shake. "Which was exactly what Miriam was doing. They were on the same team. So there was no reason why he should have been receiving out of hours messages, particularly ones he had to conceal from her. Unless"—he shrugged—"they were personal messages."

I smiled. "That kind of personal message might get you stabbed with a kitchen knife. In the States, it might get you shot with a gun purchased at the local convenience store. But it won't get you killed with a dart fired from a compressed air rifle."

He nodded a few times. "Shot. Fired with gunpowder. From a bow or an air rifle, it would be shot."

"Right, shot. But shot or fired, it looks like he was selling information."

"It does rather, doesn't it? Hard to explain it any other way."

Gallin made a face that said she wasn't satisfied. "If he was selling that kind of information, why kill him? That kind of intelligence is gold dust these days. Also, he'd be selling it to Iran or some other Islamic group. They just shoot you in the head or decapitate you. They don't play around with fancy air rifles."

"I agree," I said. "Another possibility is that he discovered somebody else was selling intelligence and was preparing to expose them. They found out and shot him."

Sir Lacklan nodded at the file in front of him. "It is possible that somebody tried to recruit him, and he played along, hoping to gather information about them, but his lack of experience betrayed him. He was very young."

I grunted. It was possible. "We'd like to go and talk to his colleagues at GCHQ."

"I assumed you would. I've made the arrangements." He turned his gaze on Gallin, who was still standing by the window. "Your father tells me there was concern at Glilot. Intelligence concerning certain operations seemed to be reaching Iran."

She was quiet for a moment. "Not just Iran. Israel has one principal enemy: Islam. Islam is as divided as the Arab people. Most of the time, they couldn't arrange a booze up in a brewery, but it seems one thing unites them, and that is the obsession with the annihilation of the Jewish people. Intelligence regarding Israeli movements seems to be reaching what's left of Hamas, as well as Hezbollah, Iran, and possibly farther afield."

I frowned at her. "What does that mean?"

"I'm not read in on the details, but it looks like Russia is monitoring our movements and has advance knowledge that could only come from inside."

"From the Institute?"

She shook her head. "We don't think so. We think it's coming from the Five Eyes."

Sir Lacklan's sigh was almost a groan. "We agree. And it's possible David was either the source of that intelligence or as you say, Alex, stumbled on that source and was eliminated."

He slid a large, fairly thick envelope across the desk toward me.

"Here you have a contact at GCHQ. She'll be expecting you, but give her a call on this number to arrange where and when to meet. That way she'll know it's you and you come from me, as it were."

I picked up the envelope and inspected it with a certain amount of skepticism.

"There are things you just can't improve on, like the knife and the hammer, unchanged through millennia because they had achieved perfection. The old-fashioned password is one of those things." I considered him across the desk. He was considering me back. I said, "I have never trusted electronics. And every year I trust them less."

"I agree. Entia non sunt multiplicanda praeter necesi-tatem. Occam's Razor, often mistranslated as the simplest answer is usually the right one. A closer translation would be don't overcomplicate things. However, today, electronics, and in particular artificial intelligence, are the order of the day. So we are required to use them."

We had a moment of silent communication, and I went to stand.

"Thank you, Sir Lacklan. We'll report back to you, in person."

As I stood, he said, "How's Nero?"

"He's well. He sends regards."

"They broke the mold after they made him."

I smiled. "He probably broke it himself."

"In our profession, trust does not come easy. But your chief is one of the few men I would truly trust in this world. He is an honest man."

"He is that."

We left and made our way down to Gallin's Jaguar. She climbed behind the wheel, and as I slammed my door, she leaned her chin on her hands on the steering wheel.

"We have the same job here, Mason."

I frowned at her. "Mm-hmm."

"But you have an extra job, one more than me."

"Yeah? What's that?"

"Keep me cold." I didn't answer. She fired up the beast and put it in gear. "Rage is a powerful motive force, Mason." As we pulled away, she added, "And people who tell you hatred is a negative emotion don't know what the hell they are talking about."

I gave my head a small twitch. "I could answer you, but I'm guessing you need to talk."

Apparently, she didn't hear me. She went on. "It is not negative to hate genocide. It is not negative to hate cruelty, or torture, or the mutilation and beheading of children.

Hating that is not negative. It is positive. Hatred is nothing more, Mason, than a powerful drive to change an existing situation. Am I wrong?"

"No."

"It has no moral value in itself, right? It is just a drive. A powerful drive. But a powerful drive like that can fog the mind."

She pulled into the traffic headed west toward Ealing and the M40, apparently using nothing more than her sixth sense. She sure as hell didn't use any of the five standard ones.

"But love—you know, they call that a positive emotion, but nothing fogs the mind more than love. *Nothing!* Love of your kids, love of family, love of country—love of a man! It fogs the mind, makes you burn." She clenched her fist, then looked at me. "You have to keep me cold."

"Oh."

She scowled at me. "What?"

"I thought maybe I could make you burn. But keeping you cold is okay too."

"Asshole."

"You are asking me to keep you objective."

"When I decide some guy, or woman, has been feeding intel to Hamas, you are going to need to sit on me until it is proven beyond any doubt."

"I hear you."

We drove in silence for a while. When we got to Marble Arch, I said, "So when it's proven beyond any doubt, do I have to get off, or can I keep sitting on you?"

She studied me for a while, glancing at me as we made

our way around toward Edgware Road. "That is so inappropriate, Mason."

"Right?"

"You are such an asshole sometimes."

"I know, right?"

"You know, you come across at first like this sophisticated, educated guy with class, but underneath…" She trailed off, shaking her head.

"Thanks." I smiled. "You also have this air of elegant sophistication, which is totally misleading."

As I spoke, I opened the envelope Sir Lacklan had given me and pulled out a single sheet of paper, two slim manila files, and one thick one which contained account details for what looked like six people. The sheet of paper had a name on it, Fiona Rider, and a telephone number that didn't look like any telephone number I had ever seen. The files were detailed abstracts of reports on David and Miriam.

"He's given us a little bit extra here. I wonder why he didn't say so."

"You going to call?"

I nodded, leafing through the file on David. Nothing leapt out at me. I called Fiona. She answered at the first ring.

"Alex Mason?"

"Are you Fiona Rider?"

She laughed prettily. "I *am!*"

"Then I am Alex Mason. How's that for synchronicity? Where and when shall we meet? We are just hitting the A40."

The laughter stopped as suddenly as it had started. "Tomorrow morning at nine sharp. I've booked you in at the

Midland. I'll send you the location and pick you up in the morning."

By the time I had thanked her, she had hung up.

ENGLAND IS A BEAUTIFUL COUNTRY. Cheltenham is not a beautiful town. And the part of Cheltenham where our inn was was probably the least lovely part of that unlovely town. To say it was dirty and dilapidated would be an insult to dirt and dilapidation. It was more a testament, a monument, to how ugly things can get when people stop giving a damn.

We parked on the Roman Road beside the inn and checked in. After that, we had lunch, bought a couple of toothbrushes, and spent the afternoon reviewing David and Miriam's abstracts. Aside from acquiring a toothbrush and drinking some good English beer, the afternoon was pretty much a washout.

Morning brought with it eggs and bacon and English pork sausages, which were surprisingly good, and after my second coffee and Gallin's mug of tea, at nine sharp, the door opened, and a woman in her early fifties with blond hair, bright eyes, and tweed pants pushed through it. She carried a purse as though it was an HK416, and her white frilly blouse and string of pearls were more like camouflage than pretty clothes.

It took her less than three seconds to spot us. She crossed the dining room grinning and holding out her arms. We stood.

"It's so good to *see* you!" she said and hugged each of us like it had been months since we'd seen each other last, instead of ever. "Sam has insisted on preparing a barbeque for lunch, but I thought I could show you around town first."

"Sounds like fun," I said with a fatuous smile, and Gallin giggled and said, "I can't wait!"

She had a VW Golf that must have been at least forty years old. We clambered in, and she took off with an admirable lack of regard for life or safety.

"Bullshit, of course," she said. "Sam's in Berlin. No barbie, I'm afraid. Not today. But take you to the Doughnut. Meet the team. David's team. Have a chat. Ay?"

She glanced at me and smiled. I smiled back. "Right. Why waste time on sub clauses? Sounds good."

"Right?"

The Doughnut was what the locals called the GCHQ building. It was a very high-tech structure built in a perfect circle. It took us less than five minutes to get there and about twice as long to clear security, even though we were accompanied by a senior officer with pretty high clearance.

When we had finally cleared the gates and made it inside the building, she led us to a bank of elevators. In theory, the Doughnut has four floors, but with the use of a biometric fob, Fiona took us down six floors into the bowels of the Earth.

"'Course it's small by your standards," she said, "But it is very sophisticated. There aren't many people we can't listen to."

She gave me a naughty wink, then gave Gallin another. The doors hissed open, and she led us down a long passage that reminded me of a set from Star Trek. We came finally to a door which opened with voice recognition and a pupil scan, and she ushered us into a conference room with an oval table and eight chairs. The door closed behind us, and she snapped, "Sit."

We sat, and she remained standing. "How's Nero?"

I studied her face a moment, then gave my head a small twitch. "Still burning Rome."

"I love that man, he's so naughty. We had an affair once, you know."

"He has a taste for exquisite things."

She smiled, but her eyes said she wanted to spank me. To Gallin, she said, "How's Daddy?"

"Did you have an affair with him, too?"

"I tried, but he wouldn't have me."

"That's not like him. How many more tests are you going to apply? It's us. You have facial recognition and now you have voice recognition."

"And psychometric and biometric. I need to know you are who you say you are. What we are looking at is no joke."

I said, "What are we looking at?"

She pulled out a chair at the end of the table and sat.

"From what we could tell, intelligence was being leaked from somewhere inside GCHQ directly to Iran, and from there, it was being disseminated to Israel's more direct enemies." She glanced at Gallin and looked almost apologetic. "Unfortunately, Israel is reluctant to work with us—"

"That might have something to do with the growing anti-Semitism in this country and the growing support for those nations who want to exterminate us."

I interrupted. "You're talking in the past tense. What's changed?"

She winced. "Frankly, we don't know. We cannot isolate

a leak within Cheltenham. We thought for a while it might be David or Miriam—"

"Did you eliminate him?"

She looked incredulous. "With a dart from a dart gun? In the first place, Mr. Mason, we need a lot more than a suspicion to resort to assassination, and in the second place, we don't need to go to such fanciful lengths. We have some pretty good professionals on hand, you know."

I grunted. "So—"

"Mr. Mason, if you please, allow me to finish what I was saying. We thought at first that it might be David or Miriam because often as not the intelligence that leaked was related to their department. However, his death makes something of a nonsense of that, as does the fact that from what we can gather, the leaks continue."

I frowned. "How can you know that?"

Gallin said, "Because they spy on us too, even though we are supposed to be allies." She turned to Fiona. "What was it, an anarchist from Cyprus? Or some dedicated bouncer NTAC?"

"Well, in this case, Captain Gallin, it's just as well that we do occasionally have a look at what's going on in the Med and the Middle East. Because we have established that intelligence originating at GCHQ is indeed still reaching Iran and her terrorist groups, and we have no idea how. MI5 are looking for leaks at home and SIS are looking in the Middle East to try and establish where it is being received, but so far, we have drawn a blank. Our one lead was David, but it looks as though we were quite wrong there."

I asked, "You think he had stumbled on the source and was eliminated?"

"Rather looks that way, doesn't it?"

Gallin leaned her elbows on the table with her hands clasped. "His cell phone was wiped clean. Even the processing system was gone. We found this morning the same thing had been done to his computer. Do you know anything about that?"

She gave a slow nod. "His mobile and his computer were secure devices. Even we couldn't have performed such a thorough cleansing so quickly. And that is alarming. Because it means we are facing a technologically highly advanced enemy. As far as I know, only the Chinese come anywhere close to that kind of sophistication. But..."

She spread her hands, and Gallin supplied the missing words.

"What the hell are the Chinese doing helping Iran against Israel?"

Fiona looked at me. "Nero thinks it might be an attempt by the Chinese to provoke a wide-ranging war in which they would be nominally neutral and could readjust the balance of power in the Middle East. China has an extremely strong industrial base; she would win out in a conflict like that. Much as the States replaced Britain after World War Two."

I glanced at Gallin. She said, "That would spell the end of Israel."

THREE

WE TALKED SOME MORE, AND SHE LEFT, SAYING David had had three colleagues aside from Miriam on the Israel team, and she would send each one of them in by turns. She gave us a list of their names and told us background files had already been emailed to us.

The first was Raj. The door slid open, and he stepped in, smiling a smile he had prepared beforehand. If you were casting a nerd for a TV sitcom, you'd want to model him on Raj. Gallin smiled at him and pointed to a chair across from her at the table.

"Grab a seat, Raj." And as he sat, she said, "Do you know why you're here?"

He spread his hands. "In very general terms." His English was accentless and spoke of an expensive education.

"Why don't you outline those general terms for me?"

"We are extremely good, Captain Gallin, at keeping secrets within the Doughnut. But within the Doughnut, rumors do seep and spread. Not major, top secret stuff, clearly. That is tightly compartmentalized on a need to know basis. But word was getting around that Islamic fundamentalists in Jordan, Lebanon, and Syria were receiving intel from Iran that could only have originated with us. I don't know how much truth there is in it." He gestured at us both. "But the fact that you are here suggests there is at least *some*."

She was quiet for a beat, then said, "The intelligence doesn't only originate in GCHQ, Raj. It originates in your team. Was that part of the rumor?"

"Really?" He said it in a kind of dead voice. Then, "No, I didn't know that."

"Tell me about David and Miriam."

He gave his shoulders a small lift. "They are—were— nice guys. They didn't socialize much. I don't think they'd been married long, and they were still into each other. We'd tease them sometimes, and David would joke that they were Jewish and family-orientated."

"That's a joke?"

If it was intended to unnerve him, it didn't work. He just smiled and said, "He intended it as one. As an explanation for why they didn't socialize much."

"Tell me, Raj, are you aware of any anti-Semitism among your colleagues? Was David anti-Semitic?"

He placed both hands very carefully on the table in front of him. "Well," he said, "that is two questions, so let me take them in turn. I am not personally aware of any anti-Semitic feelings here. That does not mean there aren't any, but as you can imagine, in an environment like this, where security is so strict and sensitive, people are not going to express racist feelings or opinions, particularly relating to Israel and/or Islam. As to Dave"—he grinned—"see my previous answer.

But in addition, he and Miriam are both Jewish. As far as I know, she at least is a practicing Jew. So I doubt very much he was anti-Semitic."

She drew breath to ask another question, but he cut her short.

"Captain Gallin, may I offer you an opinion?"

"Sure."

"It would be very difficult, and very risky, to target and recruit somebody as an informant in GCHQ based on their ideology. I mean, unless you knew them from childhood or college. Once we come in here, we become highly and intensely conditioned to be very, very careful about expressing any kind of controversial opinions." He gave a small laugh. "Or opinions that might hint at a controversial opinion. I mean, it's like that in the UK anyway, isn't it? Nobody expresses an opinion in public unless they are drunk or don't care about being labeled as some kind of reactionary. I mean you can lose your job or even go to prison."

He paused. She blinked, and he went on.

"Well, here it's like that but on steroids. We receive the data, we analyze it, and we pass it to the designated recipients. We are not going to be approached on the basis of our personal ideologies because, if we have any left, we are not going to tell anyone." He paused again. "If anyone has been turned, it was not for ideology. It was for money."

I spoke to him for the first time. "You seem real sure of that, Raj. How come?"

"I have thought about it, obviously. When the rumors started going around about the leak, I spent some time thinking about it." He frowned and averted his eyes for a moment. It was an oddly sad expression on his face. "England, Britain, the UK—it doesn't even know what to call itself anymore. It is no longer a place that inspires patriotism or loyalty. It is, ironically perhaps, the exact opposite of Israel. Where Israel fights each day to preserve its existence, England is a country that hates itself and apologizes compulsively for its existence. It is sad, in a country that has been the source of so much enlightened thought and progress in the world. But that is the way it is. Ideology is unlikely to be the source of the leak, at least at this end. The buyers will be ideologues, no doubt, but the seller will be after money. That is my opinion."

"Are you a patriot, Raj?"

He smiled, then gave a small laugh. "Oddly enough, I am. When India plays England in cricket, I am afraid I root for India, but I am not displeased on the rare occasions when England wins. But in football and rugby, I get quite emotional in support of England. I consider her my country and my home. She is like a sad, ailing nanny."

Gallin said, "Would you fight to defend her?"

"If I had to, of course."

"And if you suspected a colleague of selling information to an enemy power, would you report them?"

"Of course, without hesitation."

I said, "Raj, you realize we will want to check your accounts to see if you have received payments other than your salary. Would you allow us to do that without resorting to a court order?"

Again he gave his small laugh. "I have no objection, Mr. Mason, though I know you have already done that. When you take a job like this, you know that sort of thing comes with the territory. It's in the contract. I am at your disposal."

We talked a little more without much result, and he left.

I leaned back in my chair and spread my hands. Gallin shook her head while she scrolled through her phone.

"Next is either Tracy Fletcher, with an IQ of one hundred and fifty-five, or Martin Braun with an A-U, not an O-W. He's the team leader."

"German."

"Huh, those guys."

I didn't ask her what she meant because I was pretty sure I knew. Five minutes later, the door opened again, and Tracy Fletcher walked in. She was maybe five seven, overweight and lacking in all the things that fresh air and sunlight provide, including joy and grace. I gestured to a chair and said, "Hi, please sit down."

She gave a sneaky smile, like she was laughing inside at some private joke that we were too stupid to understand, and sat. I dove right in.

"Would you consider yourself a patriot, Tracy?"

Her eyes flitted over my face, and her mouth sagged slightly, like she was having trouble believing how stupid my question was.

"This is GCHQ. If you ask anyone here that question, they have to tell you they are or they lose their job. Because this is, uh, GCHQ?"

I gave her a smile that was bland. "Okay, now that we have cleared up how stupid the question is, would you please answer it?"

She stifled a sigh. "Yeah, I am, as it happens. More than some."

I turned my smile on Gallin. "What do you know? I learned something from my question."

"Why am I being questioned by an American?" It was Tracy. I kept the smile on my face and told her, "Because your boss told you to be. Would you consider Raj and Miriam to be patriotic?"

"That's two different questions."

I suppressed a sigh. "I know how many questions it is, Tracy. And you can answer them in any order you like. Now, please."

"Raj says he is, and probably believes he is, but when push comes to shove, he is an Indian. It's not an issue because right now and for the foreseeable future, India is an ally. But if the balance of power shifts beyond a critical point, India will be absorbed into the East, and his loyalties will go with it." Her eyes traveled around the walls and the ceiling. "If he is informed of my opinion, it will seriously damage the cohesion of our team."

I blinked at her and asked, "What about Miriam?"

"She's English by birth going back generations, but she is above and beyond anything else Jewish. She has an Israeli passport as well as an English one, and her loyalties are very firmly with Israel. I don't blame her. Mine would be too. Now I suppose you'll want to know about David."

"Are you familiar with the rumors that were circulating about him?"

"That he was selling intelligence to the Russians or the Iranians? Yes."

"What do you make of them?"

"Well, somebody is. And David had all the backbone of a mature salp."

Gallin looked interested. "Yeah? What makes you say that?"

She didn't answer right away. She was silent, giving her head small, irregular shakes, like she was disagreeing with some inner dialogue.

"October seventh," she said suddenly. "Miriam was in tears. It was so bad her supervisor asked if she wanted to go home. She said no, our work was now more important than ever, and she stayed at her post, working while she was wiping tears from her eyes. You know what *he* was on about?"

"Tell me."

"How he could get to the next level in a computer game he was playing. He just didn't care. This was his"—she faltered, like the expression of strong emotion was unnatural to her—"his ancestral home, the home of his people, he had family and cousins there, but he just didn't care."

I frowned. "How did Miriam react to David's indifference?"

She shrugged. "She didn't. At work, they pretty much ignored each other. Everything is about compartments here. This is the brain of the hive. Or one of them, anyway."

Gallin said, "You seem to sympathize with Israel. You have some connection?"

She lifted her chin slightly. It struck me how pale she looked. She said, "No," then she gave a goofy grin and seemed to duck her head. "Unless having posters of Gal Gadot all over my walls counts as a connection."

Gallin laughed, and I couldn't help smiling. Tracy turned serious.

"Someone once said to me, if you remove any two

nations from the history of humanity, that removal will have a greater or lesser impact, but the general direction will be the same. But remove the British and the Jews, and we never get past the Renaissance, we never develop empirical science and psychology, and we never get off the surface of the planet." She paused. Her cheeks flushed. "Naturally I don't agree with that point of view. That would be unacceptable and offensive to other nations, but nevertheless, it is thought-provoking."

My eyebrows had scaled their way to my hairline. I said, "Very."

"It's a point of view." She gave that funny, superior smile again. "It makes me laugh when people accuse the Jews of using banking to take over the world. Nobody ever accuses the English of that, but it's what we did. I mean, we practically own the Federal Reserve, don't we?"

We asked her a few more questions, but by then I had decided she was an interesting person, but not a person of interest.

Just before she got up to leave, she paused.

"I know you'll be going through our financial records with a fine-toothed comb. In fact, you've probably done it already. The assumption is, all too often these days, that we, the English, have no national loyalty anymore. We all have a pathological hatred of our own country." She held my eye. "That's why you asked me about patriotism. We'd all sell our country down the line for enough money. But it's not true. The silent majority, the ones who are actually English, still love their country. If there has been betrayal or treason, it was ideologically motivated, by our enemies."

She stood and moved to the door. There she paused.

"I don't know what arrangements you've made, but Martin called in sick this morning."

Then she turned and left. I stared at the closed door. Then I stared at Gallin. "He called in sick." I stood. "Let's go!"

But she was already on her feet, reaching for the door. As she opened it and we stepped out, we saw Fiona's silhouette hurrying up the corridor toward us.

"I've sent a car to his house." Like we'd been in telepathic communication. "He's here in Chelmsford."

"I've got his address." I kind of growled it at her as I pushed past. "Call your man off. I don't want anyone in his house till we get there. Get us back to the hotel. Your man is probably halfway around the world by now."

"I've called you a car."

I stopped and turned to her. "I want his computer sealed. I want every piece of his hardware sealed. His chair, his table, his pens. Everything. Odin will send a team. Do not touch anything."

Her face went like cement. "You have no authority—"

"Can it. Sir Lacklan Orme will confirm it, and so will Nero."

I pulled my cell and made for the door with Fiona on my heels.

"Sir Lacklan, Martin Braun called in sick today. I'm on my way to his house. Fiona needs your authorization to seal his chair and desk and all his IT equipment. Can you talk to her? I need to call Nero."

I hung up. Gallin was already calling Nero. We pushed out the doors where there was a Range Rover waiting.

Fiona's cell started ringing. I told her, "I'll be in touch. If you have some way of tracking him, track him."

"I'll try. But he'll know we're doing it."

"Try."

I pulled open the door. Gallin handed me her cell as she was climbing in. I got in, and we took off. Nero was his usual self.

"Report."

"Martin Braun called in sick this morning."

"You are going to his house?"

"Yes."

"Where are you now?"

"In a GCHQ Range Rover on my way to the hotel."

"Call me when you have finished at the house. Find out where he has gone."

"Ten-four."

"Alex?"

"Yes, sir."

"You are not a policeman. Try to avoid such vulgarities in future."

"You got it, sir."

He sighed and hung up just as we pulled up at the hotel.

FOUR

Martin Braun lived at the corner of Brooklyn Gardens. It was a two-story 1930s house with a gabled roof and bow windows, set back from the road at the end of a concrete drive. In the drive there was a red Ford Puma. At the back of the house, there was a park with a small woodland.

Dehan pulled into the drive and parked, obstructing the exit for the Puma, and we both climbed out. She glanced around before making for the door.

"If you were hoping to dodge the roving eye of artificial intelligence, would you go for a place like this?"

"Reckon I might."

She leaned on the bell while I scanned the windows. The drapes were all drawn. Maybe the sunlight hurt his eyes.

I walked to the back of the house and tried the kitchen door. It was locked, and the drapes there were closed too. I made my way back to the front. Gallin asked me the question with a face and a jerk of her chin. I answered with a shake of my head. I pulled my cell and called Fiona.

"Can you deactivate Martin's alarm?"

She was silent for a long moment. Her silence said she didn't like it. A brief sigh and then, "Yes. I've already taken care of it."

I gave Gallin the nod and told Fiona, "Thanks."

Gallin reached in her pocket, pulled out a Swiss Army knife, and selected the screwdriver. She gave it a practiced thump and a twist, and the door swung in.

Silence comes in two shades. There is a slightly richer shade when someone in the silence is keeping very still and trying not to breathe. And then there is that grayer shade when the silence is the product of emptiness. That was the silence that greeted us as we moved over the threshold.

Gallin closed the door behind us. She already had her P226 in her hand. I said, "This ain't proof yet, you know that."

"I know that. You want to take upstairs?"

"There's nobody here."

"I know." She toed open the door to the living room. "But he left something that said where he was going. He left it down here, or he left it upstairs." She looked me in the eye. "You take upstairs, and I'll look down here."

I arched an eyebrow at her. "Yessah." And as I climbed the stairs, I quoted ZZ Top at the steps. "I got twenny-five lighters on my dresser, yessah! *Yes*-sah!"

Upstairs had a bathroom with a walk-in shower, one small bedroom, two medium-sized and one large with an en suite bathroom with a shower and a Jacuzzi. His toothbrush was there, with the toothpaste, his hairbrush, shampoo, razor, and moisturizer. I curled my lip. I could hear Gallin in my head saying, "Never trust a man who uses moisturizer."

The small bedroom was a junk room, but a good scrounge found nothing of interest. Two of the bedrooms were spares, and they gave up nothing either, except that one of the wardrobes held an empty shoe box that smelled of gun oil.

His wardrobe and his chests of drawers were almost full, but you got the feeling there were some essentials missing. He'd run and tried to hide the fact, that much was clear, but there was nothing to say where he'd run to. I went back down the stairs.

When I got to the kitchen, Gallin was staring in the fridge.

"Does the hummus suggest to you he went to Cyprus?"

"Middle East generally, Mason. I thought you'd know that."

"You're not a happy bunny, are you, Gallin?"

"Right now I am not any kind of bunny." She slammed the door and moved past me. I stood staring at the items beside the stove: a mug, a kettle, a saucer holding a used teabag, and a tannin-stained teaspoon. Above them a couple of cupboards. Beneath them two drawers, and beneath those more cupboards.

"Did you check the cutlery drawer?"

Her voice came from the living room. "What for, a knife to cut my wrists? I'm not there yet, but give me five minutes."

I hunkered down and worked my way through the pots

and pans in the lower cupboards. I heard a voice behind me asking, "What the hell are you looking for in there?"

"If I knew," I said, removing the lid from a large pot, "I probably wouldn't be looking here."

"I would have thought, you know, things like papers, correspondence, computers..." Her voice faded toward the front of the house. "...that crazy kind of thing..." then less distinctly, muttering, "...pots and pans..."

I stood and made my way systematically through the tea, instant coffee, oats, spaghetti, and red kidney beans. Then I went through the bottom drawer, where the batteries, masking tape, old screws, and nameless plastic objects in transparent plastic bags are kept. The next one up had those barbeque utensils you receive for a Christmas present and never use. The second from the top was kitchen towels and gingham napkins, and the top one was cutlery in a plastic tray that was slightly too small for the drawer. There were bottle openers, corkscrews, and Parmesan cheese graters beside it. At the front of the drawer, there was a pair of kitchen scissors, a pastry brush, and a wooden pestle piled on top of each other.

I was about to close it again, but for the sake of completeness, and maybe because the pestle, the brush, and the scissors looked just a little too cramped and it was just a little too overcrowded to see right to the back, I pulled out the drawer and set it on the surface beside the stove. And just behind the plastic tray was a slightly scrunched manila envelope.

I let a smug smile leach into my voice and called out, "Does an envelope count as paper?"

I picked it up and lifted the flap. Gallin's voice behind me said, "What?"

I said, "It's empty. But it's an odd place to have a manila envelope."

I heard her approaching behind me. I squeezed in the sides so that it gaped and peered inside, then felt in with my fingers.

"There is a difference in the texture of the paper..."

"What are you talking about, Mason? What is it with the kitchen?"

"Men think it's a place nobody ever goes," I said absently. I could feel the roughness of the manila paper, and then it became silky and smooth. I picked at it with my nail and carefully pulled out a blue five-hundred peso note and held it up for her to see.

"It's brand new and had stuck to the side of the envelope. He must have pulled the rest out in a hurry, and this one got left behind. See, Gallin, when you can't find something, that usually means it ain't where you expect it to be. So then, what you do is, you look where you *don't* expect it to be."

"You're an asshole, Mason. You're smart, but you're an asshole."

"I would hazard a wild guess, Gallin, that he is going to Mexico." I shrugged and spread my hands. "If you think I am wrong and should draw a different conclusion, please enlighten me."

"Asshole. Mexico covers seven hundred and sixty thousand six hundred and ten square miles. What that five hundred peso bill does not tell us, Mason"—she punched me gently on the chest—"is in which one of those seven hundred and sixty thousand six hundred and ten square miles Martin Braun is going to be."

"The world," I told her, "covers one hundred and ninety six point nine *million* square miles, wiseass. So I think," I said, and slapped the five hundred peso bill against her bosom, "I have narrowed the search down a little."

Her eyes became hooded, but I could tell she was fighting a grin. "Watch where you put your money, big guy."

I tucked the money in where it looked cozy and pulled my cell from my pocket. It rang once, and Nero said, "Report."

"No. I need information urgently. Direct flights to Mexico from London. Martin Braun is probably flying to Mexico. Wherever he's going, we are probably in time to intercept him."

"Wait."

Gallin and I stared at each other while I waited. She removed the bill from her shirt, and I put the phone on speaker. Nero said, "Cancun from Gatwick, Mexico City from Heathrow. What's to stop him going to Amsterdam, Paris, Madrid, Brussels, and flying from there?"

"Nothing, except that it delays him and increases his risk of being caught. If he got the pesos here, he intended to fly from here."

"What pesos?"

"Never mind, sir. I'll report shortly. Right now, we need agents looking for Braun at Cancun and Mexico city on flights from London over the next twenty-four to forty-eight hours."

"What pesos?"

"He had an envelope in his cutlery drawer with a five hundred peso bill stuck in it."

"What does your gut tell you? Mexico City or Cancun? Captain Gallin, your opinion also."

We spoke at the same time. "Cancun." I added, "Tourist friendly, less security, and easier to get lost in the crowd."

"Agreed. Go to Cancun—now. Get luggage. Go to the Kempinsky. Do not be conspicuous."

I hung up and dialed Fiona. While it rang, I said to Gallin, "You want to arrange the tickets and the hotel?"

She was writing on her phone. "Way ahead of you, big guy." She paused and frowned at me. "Odin's paying, right? You have like a trillion dollar black budget. Shall we get the bridal suite or the imperial suite?"

"Yes, Mason, this is Fiona. Any news?"

"He's gone to Mexico. We're going after him."

"Mexico? Jesus Christ!"

"You need to get your forensic guys in here. It looks like he left in a hurry. So he might have been careless. Send me the report when you have it, will you? Along with the report on David's apartment."

"Will do."

And we locked up the house and headed off to buy luggage that would be inconspicuous at the five-star Kempinsky in Cancun.

———

Martin Braun was in fact at Gatwick Airport. He was at his departure gate sitting on an uncomfortable plastic chair suffering each minute as though it were an hour of agony with some bastard pouring sulfuric acid into his belly. Had any of the people around him given a damn, they might have noticed a man whose complexion was pasty and pale with the texture of damp wax, whose pupils were little more than pinpricks, and whose breathing spoke of an accelerated heartbeat. But the people around him were on their way to Cancun, to get drunk, try to get laid, and suffer hangovers and disappointment in the morning sun on the white sands of *Playa Delfines*, and they didn't give a damn about him or anybody else. In fact, he thought sourly as he observed them, the reason they were not going to get laid in their thudding nightclubs—aside from being too drunk to deliver anything firmer than overcooked macaroni—was because they could not detach themselves from their screens long enough to notice there was another human being beside them.

His anxiety and his mood darkened. Perhaps, he told himself, they didn't need to notice because they were all connected, like wasps or ants, sharing a common consciousness through their phones. They were evolving, in some grotesque way, into AI biological terminals. It was like *The Invasion of the Body Snatchers*, only instead of replacing the body, they reprogrammed the individual's brain to become a component part of a global mind.

A mind that was not sentient but digital, that saw the human being as a transitory necessity with limited use and a limited shelf life.

The drones, because that was how he saw them, had started gathering into a line to start boarding, following the instructions issued by the disembodied electronic voice. If you wanted people to obey, you did not shout or scream or give orders. What people obeyed at what was almost a genetic level was a disembodied electronic voice.

He waited until the line was almost finished. Then he pulled his passport, in the name of John Smith, and his boarding pass from his leather hand luggage and boarded the plane.

Nobody stopped him, nobody scrutinized him, nobody even noticed him. That was par for the course. He was, and always had been, the man nobody noticed. Not so much gray as opaque.

But he noticed everything. His mind was not controlled and managed from outside. He was the master of his own mind. Attention, concentration, observation. That was his holy trinity, and as he moved down the cramped aisle, he noted and read every face, every expression, every glance.

He came to his seat and shoved his bag into the overhead locker. As he did it, he repeated to himself over and over, "I am, I am *I*. I am, I am unique, I am I, I am I."

The mantra eased him. They might kill him, they might destroy him, but they would *never* own him.

Never.

He took his seat and pulled his cell from his pocket. He dialed and held the phone to his ear. It was answered after the third ring.

"Hi, Sue, it's Martin. Listen, I've picked up some kind of stomach bug or something. All night in the damned loo. Tell Fi I'll call her this p.m., will you? I really need to sleep."

"All right, Martin. I'll tell her. Get better."

.   .   .

THE FLIGHT WAS long and tedious, and though he managed to sleep fitfully, the anxiety never left him completely. His rational mind, which he thought of as his audio-digital process, told him there was no way the authorities would be able to track him, much less identify him as John Smith. But his emotional mind, which he thought of as his kinesthetic process, was by definition irrational and saw the scene played out over and over as he walked through passport control and they closed in on him. It might be uniformed men or they might be plainclothes.

Or they might be just a couple of men in suits who brushed against him, and in minutes he would be dead.

All over, no more pain or anxiety or suffering.

It would be a release if they did it like that, but he wasn't ready for it. Not yet.

At Cancun, the line for passport control was not long, but it seemed interminable. When he finally handed over his passport, the official studied it like he'd never seen one before and didn't understand how it worked. After a long moment, he turned and studied Martin's face for an embarrassingly long time. Maybe he was suspicious of his sweating brow or his pinprick pupils or the fact that he kept swallowing every fifteen seconds.

"What is the reason for your visit to Mexico?"

"Just a holiday, pleasure..."

"Where you are staying?"

"At the..." For horrific, unendurable seconds he could not remember the name of the hotel. "The..." He stared at the official and grinned a horrible rictus. "The, The Hotel Bahari." He laughed too loud. "I'm sorry. It's been a long flight. Hotel Bahari, Road C and Quintana."

"You have reservation?" He jerked his chin at Martin's jacket, like he should have the reservation in there somewhere. Martin had expected it and reached in his inside pocket, but his hand was trembling as he handed it over. The official took it, gave him a once-over, stamped his passport, and handed it all back.

"Enjoy your stay in Cancun," he said, like he really didn't mean it.

Martin made his way to the toilets, retched for a couple of minutes, wept for a couple more, then rinsed his mouth and made his way out to arrivals. Nobody brushed against him, nobody was waiting for him, and nobody intercepted him.

He moved through the crowds of floral-shirted Americans and walked out onto the sidewalk. Over on his left was the taxi rank.

He slung his bag on the back seat and told the driver, "Hampton Inn, Boulevard Luis Donaldo. You know it? Habla Ingles?"

The driver flicked ash out the window. "I know," he said. "I speakin' English."

After a fifteen-minute drive, they arrived at the Hampton Inn, and the cab pulled up outside the main entrance. He paid the driver and clambered out, dragging his bag after him. Then he stood and watched as the cab drove away. When it was out of sight, he pulled his cell from his pocket. Through the plate glass doors of the Hampton, he could see a girl in a blue uniform watching him. He ignored her and ordered another cab. This one would take him to his real hotel on the Kukulcan Boulevard. It was a tourist hotel out on the lagoon. Tourist hotels had the big advantage of a high turnover of residents and staff, so the chances of going unnoticed were that much higher.

He stowed his John Smith passport in his bag and pulled out the one he'd used to make the reservation. This one was in the name of Peter Clark. His hands had stopped trembling now, his sweating had eased, and his breathing was starting to settle. He was starting to believe that maybe, just maybe, he might get away.

FIVE

WE HAD PICKED UP THE COMPANY GULFSTREAM, A long-range G700, at City Airport and settled in for the eight-hour flight. British security had reported negative on any sightings of Martin leaving any British airport, which was not a surprise as he almost certainly had a false passport, and in any case, as Gallin had observed, "He called in sick while he was boarding the plane. Last thing he did before going to airplane mode. It's what I'd have done."

Officers at Mexico and Cancun had not spotted him arriving, either, which was disappointing but not that surprising either. A guy heading a team of analysts specializing in Islam and Israel at GCHQ could be expected to have a brain and, if not craft skills, at least enough know-how to get through an airport without being spotted.

I was sitting at the highly polished table, sipping a martini and leafing through the passenger lists for the last six flights from Gatwick to Cancun. Gallin was perusing her own copies, but she was stretched out on the sofa with her ankles crossed and her lips pursed. I tossed the papers on the table and sighed.

"There is no Martin Braun, and the only MJ is Michael Jenkins, who is eighty-two years old. If he was on one these flights—*if* he was on one of these flights, a big if—he could be any one of the almost nine hundred men on those flights."

"No," she said absently.

I gave her a disagreeable look which she didn't see because she didn't look back. So I had to say "*Oh?*" with labored sarcasm.

She did a one-shouldered shrug and said, "Pui Kwan Kay, Bemnet Tesfaye, Jonah Koroi, Uh..."

"I get it. He looks English, and a lot of people on those planes don't."

"Right, but I'm not being funny, Mason. In fact, I was counting when you interrupted me." She twisted and arched her back so she could look at me and smile. "You're talking about maybe fifty percent of these male travelers could not have been Martin."

"It's challenging grammar, but I understand. And still, that still leaves us with four hundred or four fifty—"

She swung her legs off the sofa and came and sat opposite me at the table.

"C'mon, big guy. Get your head out of your martini and think. Martin Braun is thirty-six. So you eliminate all those over forty and all those under thirty. What's that, another thirty percent, approximately? That leaves you maybe ninety passengers. Of those, we focus on the two flights that are most closely within the time frame he was most likely to travel. That gives us—"

"Thirty passengers. And okay, you're right and that's clever yadda yadda, but it is still thirty passengers we have no—"

"Twenty-five."

"What?"

"Twenty-five. Ten on one flight and fifteen on the other. And we can reduce them further." She shoved two sheets of paper in front of me and started pointing at names. "This guy was obese, and we know Martin ain't. These two guys are married, and they are traveling together. These *four* were going to a stag party and were traveling first class." She gave a short laugh. "*These* guys are doctors attending a conference and—"

"Gallin."

"What?"

"How many did you actually boil it down to?"

"Seven, on the Gatwick to Cancun flight that departed four hours after they got the news that David had been killed and fifteen minutes after Fiona's secretary got the call saying Martin was sick."

"I don't know. Maybe I love you. Maybe I hate you. The jury is still out." She had a stupid grin on her face. I said, "You've narrowed it down more, haven't you?"

She shrugged. "You tell me, Mr. Mason, ODIN big shot I-Found-Five-Hundred-Pesos-in-the-Cutlery-Drawer.   We have"—she gave a little cough to clear her throat—"Benjamin Rowbotham, Edward Billings, Bruce Fanshawe, Alexander Percival-Hastings, Simon Lovelock, Cyril Merryweather..."

"And?"

"John Smith."

I sighed and gazed out at the clouds. The setting sun was touching their tips with gold.

"Tell me you're kidding."

"The most common names in Britain are the same as the most common names in the States: Smith, Jones, Williams, Taylor... But there are maybe six hundred thousand Smiths out of sixty million people, or half a million Joneses, in all of the UK. Take a random sample of men, and you're not *that* likely to find a Smith, and much less a John Smith. For my money, he was overcautious. Among two hundred and fifty or three hundred passengers he was invisible, but when you narrow it down to white, Anglo-Saxon men between thirty and forty, he stands out like a sore thumb."

"That is..." I sighed yet again. "Okay, it is very clever, but it is one hell of a reach, Gallin."

"Yeah, you're right."

"What?"

"No, you're right, Mason. What we should do is spend the next four hours staring at these lists and moaning about how impossible the task is while we sip martinis."

"Come on!"

"No, you're right. Tell me, what should we do when we get there?" I drew breath, but she raised a hand. "No, I'll tell you. We'll get Nero to pull strings and have the Cancun police track every single one of those ninety white, Anglo-Saxon males around Cancun. Because with thirty million visitors and soaring levels of drug crime and corruption, they have nothing better to do."

"Why—"

"Hey, no, it's okay. I just spent two hours making a

detailed analysis of the situation, but it's fine. We'll do it your way."

"Why—"

She frowned and snapped her fingers a few times. "Which is... Remind me. What was your way?"

"Gallin, have a large whiskey, would you, and don't talk again till we get to Cancun. We'll check out John Smith before anybody else. I still say it's one hell of a reach. If it doesn't pay off, we'll go with plan B."

"Which is...?"

"Drink and stop talking, will you?"

She sat in silence while I went through her lists. She had been extremely methodical and, though I didn't show it, I was impressed. I had to admit she was right. The name John Smith stood out like a sore thumb. I still thought it was one hell of a reach, but I tried to remember how many John Smiths I had met in my life, and I had to admit I had not met many.

"Six hundred thousand, huh?" I frowned at her and gave my head a small shake. "Where do you get these facts from?"

She blinked once. Aside from that, she did nothing but stare at me.

"Okay, Gallin, it was a great piece of work. I will be astonished if it pays off, but I give you ten points for dedication, commitment, and method. Now will you relax and have a goddamn drink, please!"

Another silent blink.

"Okay, it's brilliant. Just getting it down to seven was brilliant in itself. John Smith..." I gave her a thumbs-up. "Brilliant!"

She smiled. It was a smug smile, and she went to get a

drink. I rolled my eyes and looked back at the list. Benjamin Rowbotham, Edward Billings, Bruce Fanshawe, Alexander Percival-Hastings, Simon Lovelock, Cyril Merryweather. It was true that the Brits often have names that sound weird to us. To them, names like Hoffstadder and Gunter sound weird. To us, it's Rowbotham and Fanshawe, but the one who stood out for me was Cyril Merryweather. It was just too English. I was aware my reasoning was the same as Gallin's, and she was actually English, so she should know. But Cyril Merryweather? I shook my head. Too much.

We touched down in Cancun at three p.m. The airport authorities had been alerted of our arrival, and we were ushered through to an office where a couple of agents from the consulate agency was waiting for us. They were in jeans and shirts with open collars and had that open, friendly smile which characterizes the modern CIA.

The older guy, who had shaggy blond hair and a beard, stepped forward, holding out his hand. "I'm Frank, this is Bob." He indicated his younger, clean-shaven pal. "We flew over from Mexico City this morning when we got the call from London."

We shook, and I told him, "Alex Mason, and this is Captain Gallin."

He handed me a fob. "You have a Caddy CTS just outside. Anything else we can do to help, let us know. You're looking for a Martin Braun? British?"

I gave him the sheet of paper with Gallin's list of seven names. Gallin spoke.

"This guy is a team leader for GCHQ. He is not traveling under his own name. We went through all the relevant passenger lists on the flight and narrowed it down to these most likely passengers."

Bob took it, and they both scrutinized it. Bob gave a small laugh. "Cyril Merryweather?"

Frank chuckled. "Right?"

I smiled at Gallin and waggled my eyebrows. To them, I said, "A first step would be to see how many of those seven guys are registered with the British Consul. Maybe none. But whoever is registered here we can be sure is not our guy. After that, we'll need to ask the cops where each of these individuals is staying. That information should be registered, either as an hotel or a private residence, right?"

Frank nodded. "Not a problem. Anything else?" I shook my head, and he tapped the paper, laughing. "If I were you, I'd start with Cyril Merryweather. That name is just, no way, man. Nobody is called that, right?"

They showed us to the car, we thanked them, and they took off in a large Chevy SUV with smoked windows that had CIA written all over it. As we watched them drive away, I said, "You don't think Cyril Merryweather...?"

"Please! This guy is a highly intelligent Mr. Anonymous. You really think he'd pick a name like that? Come on, let's go talk to the taxi drivers."

We spent half an hour talking to the taxi drivers at the rank and showing them pictures of Martin Braun. They all had the peculiar trick of raising their shoulders at the same time as they lowered the corners of their mouth. Some of them said, "Is possibol, American?"

Gallin told them, "No, Americano no, ingles."

We'd pretty much given up and were on our way back to the car when a cab came in from delivering a fare and stopped at the rear of the line. We turned and made our way back as the driver climbed out and lit up a cigarette. As we approached, he pointed to the front of the line.

"You take number one. Front of line."

Gallin shook her head and held up the picture on her cell.

"You know this guy? You give him a ride?"

His eyes lingered on the picture, then he sucked on his cigarette and shrugged. But Gallin had caught the brief pause as the slight dilation of his pupils too.

"Give me good information and you get twenty American dollars. When did you give him a ride?"

"Maybe in the morning. Maybe is him."

I asked, "How many cases?"

"No case. Joss a bag." He held out his fist like he was holding a carryon.

"Where was he going?"

His eyes drifted up to his left, which if you believe eye accessing cues meant he was remembering and not inventing. After a moment, he nodded. "Ampton Inn, Boulevard Luis Donaldo."

Gallin shoved fifty bucks in his shirt pocket and gave him the kind of look that convinces turkeys Christmas has arrived.

"You never saw us, never talked to us, never gave us any information. Comprende?"

"Comprendo."

We returned to the Caddy and took a leisurely drive up 307 as far as the Pabellon Cumbres shopping mall's giant parking lot, where the Hampton Inn is located, and pulled up outside. It was very rectangular and had a lot of glass. We climbed out of the Caddy, slammed the doors, and walked into a lobby that was all white marble and IKEA furniture. A very pretty girl with a dark blue uniform smiled at us as we approached. I gave her a big smile back.

"We are supposed to meet a friend here today, I wonder if he's checked in yet?"

She tilted her head on one side to make the smile even prettier. "What's his name?"

I glanced at Gallin and said, "Cyril Merryweather."

She giggled and asked me to spell it. I spelled it, and she checked her computer. After a while, she shook her head.

"No, he hasn't checked in, and we don't have a booking for that name either."

Gallin leaned on the counter next to me. "His friend John might have booked it. John Smith? He should have checked in this morning."

The pretty receptionist sang a little, "papam, papam papam..." while she rattled at the keyboard. Then her face lit up. "Ah! Here we are, John Smith, ummm..." She paused. "He is booked in, he reserve the room, but he never turn up. Never checked in."

Gallin laughed a little too loudly and grinned at me. "Sounds like our Johnny!"

I ignored her and frowned at the pretty receptionist. "Are you absolutely sure? Because a taxi driver told us he had brought him here."

Her frown said she thought that was odd. When Gallin showed her the photograph on her cell, she looked at the picture and then at each of us in turn.

"Are you police?"

I showed her my card. "I am with American Intelligence,

my colleague is with British Intelligence. We are here at the invitation of your government, and we are looking for this young man who might be in grave danger if we don't find him soon. Have you seen him?"

She wasn't convinced, but she looked at the picture again. After a second, she scratched her light, fluffy hair in thought.

"Well, this morning a taxi arrived, and a man got out with a bag. I thought he was going to check in, but he call another cab and left. I thought it was odd, but..." She shrugged like what could she do if something was odd? "It maybe looks like him."

Gallin asked, "Did you happen to notice the number of the cab that collected him on the door?"

She looked uncomfortable. "No, but..."

I glanced outside. "The security cameras." I leaned on the counter and gave her my nicest smile. "I could call the cops and get them to authorize it, but that would be a big inconvenience for you and would be a huge waste of time that could cost Johnny his life. Let's do it this way. I give you a hundred American dollars, you drop your pen, and while you look for it we slip in and have a look at your security footage? Win-win."

She looked uncertain. I put a hundred bucks on the counter, and she dropped her pen. She gave a sheepish smile and said, "Oops..."

And then she disappeared.

SIX

THE TAXI WAS NUMBER THIRTY-TWO AND belonged to the Sure Thing Taxi Company, which was a reminder never to use colloquialisms in a language which is not your own. The Sure Thing HQ was a couple of miles away on Calle 56, or 56th Street, so we drove there and parked outside. It was basically a large, dirty garage with an office on the right side as you entered behind a pane of glass and a broken door. You half expected to find Danny DeVito there staring up at you with a dose of attitude. As we walked in, there was a chorus of wolf whistles and "Madre mía!"

We ignored it and pushed into the office, where instead of Danny DeVito, there was a guy in a stained undershirt who had enough hair on his body to resurface a gorilla. His mustache looked like it had wildlife living in it, and the hair under his arms probably accounted for most of the dark matter in the universe. He was counting money but looked up and grunted as we came in. A small amount of ash fell from the cigarette he had in his mouth onto the bills on his desk.

"Que?"

"Habla ingles?"

"Everybody espikin English. You wanna taxi?"

"No." We sat opposite him, and I pulled out the card that said I worked for the Pentagon. I showed it to him. "I work for American Intelligence."

He threw back his head and laughed. "American intelligence! Haha! Is good." He shrugged elaborately and spread his hands. "I don't know this thing! What is?" He laughed again.

I didn't laugh with him. I waited till he'd finished. "I am here at the invitation of the Mexican government. I can call on them for help any time I need to. You understand?"

He twitched one shoulder to show he wasn't impressed. I went on. "I need to talk to the driver of taxi number thirty-two."

He gave another big, hairy, sweaty shrug and spat elaborately on the floor.

"He is no here. He comin' in tonight."

"How much will it cost for him to come in now?"

He pointed at me with his palm up, like he was Hamlet looking at Yorick's skull. "See, gringo? You no so intelligent, huh? See, I am one Mexican who no for sale. Maybe there are more. You cannot buy everythin' you want, see, gringo?"

I drew breath, but Gallin interrupted. "That's very impressive, and I am sure you are one hell of a guy. But we're looking for a man whose life is in danger, and we need to get to him soon."

"His life in danger? My life in danger too. Your life in danger. Everybody life in danger, baby. Because we all gonna die. He comin' in at nine tonight. You come you talk to him. Maybe he is for sale, eh, gringo?"

The last was directed at me with a jerk of his chin in my direction.

"Yeah, who knows." I turned to Gallin. "Come on, let's go check in. We'll come back at nine."

She looked like she hadn't heard me. She was staring hard at Mr. Hair behind his desk. Very deliberately she removed her leather jacket and handed it to me. Her shoulder holster was clearly on display, as was the butt of her Sig Sauer P226. She took a couple of steps forward and leaned on the desk. The guy had turned the color and texture of a church candle.

"What's your name?"

The guy swallowed big. "Miguel, señora, I no mean..."

"Shut up, Miguel." She said it quietly without aggression. "I am going to go away now, but I will come back. When I do, the driver of car thirty-two will be here. You know how I know that?"

He gave his head a small shake.

"I know that because, if he is not, I am going tear out your fat guts with my bare hands and lynch you with them. And I am not speaking metaphorically, Miguel. I mean it. I *need* that driver, and you will give him to me. Do you understand me?"

"Yes, señora."

She took her jacket without looking at me and shrugged it on.

"We better go and check in," she said, echoing my words from moments before, and I followed her out to the car. There she held out her hand. "Give me the key. I need to drive."

I handed her the fob. "Can we please get there alive?"

By the time I had got in and sat beside her, she still hadn't answered. "What's going on, Gallin? The guy runs a cab company. He was ugly and obnoxious, but you didn't need to threaten to kill him."

She fired up the big engine and pulled away easy.

"Give me a second," she said.

She eased onto the Avenida Cancún in an alarmingly quiet way and followed the traffic, easy and relaxed, around toward the big circus where the clock tower stands. Once we were in the flow, she raised her right index finger and started talking.

"This is not special pleading, Mason. I am just explaining."

"Okay."

"Don't talk, just listen. Please." The 'please' got my attention, so I shut up and listened. "There is not a nation on this planet that understands what it means to be a Jew. I am not going to recite our history to you. I know you know it. But I will say it goes back to the beginning of history. It's in our DNA: fight, survive, or be exterminated. You understand that instinct as a man, as an individual."

She paused a moment as we came off the circus onto Bonampak Avenue. Then she said, "We understand it as a *race*, as a culture, as a people. Each Jew, whether he is true to it or not, understands in his bones that he is responsible for every other Jew." She shrugged. "Maybe that sounds stupid or melodramatic. I don't give a shit. It's what we have learned over the centuries. It's how we survive."

"It makes sense."

She glanced at me. "Thanks." There was no irony in it. Then she added, "They beheaded four-year-old children, Mason. They did things that defy imagining. However sadistic you may be, you can't imagine things that would cause more horror or more suffering than what they did. They did these things to mothers and children."

"I know. I read the reports and saw the videos."

"And this son of a bitch, himself a Jew, is selling them intelligence so they can do it again."

I was quiet for a while as we curled around onto the Avenue of Kukulcan and began to move south with the ocean on our left, where the Gulf of Mexico meets the Caribbean Sea. The Lagoon of Love was on our right.

After a moment, I said,

"We don't know yet, Gallin, whether David and Martin were selling intelligence to Iran or whether they found out that somebody else was. You have to stay objective."

"Right."

"I am not asking, Gallin."

"I know. I'm going to find out." And she looked at me for a second or two, then gave a small smile. "But I don't aim to let a fat, greasy son of a bitch like Miguel get in my way."

"Or a thin, dry one."

"Or a thin, dry, bald one."

Gallin had booked us a seaside suite at the Kempinsky Grand Hotel, which in the good old days had been the Ritz Carlton. As we pulled into the half-moon drive, under all the flags and the palm trees, Gallin shook her head and sighed.

"The Institute doesn't put us up in places like this."

The Institute was what she called the Mossad, which is really the Institute for Intelligence and Special Operations. Mossad in Hebrew means institute.

I nodded with my mind still on what she had been saying earlier. "That's because you haven't got a trillion dollar black budget," I said, and I was only partly joking.

While we checked in, the valets skipped down and collected our inconspicuous bags. We settled in to the suite, showered and changed, and went down for a drink in the bar, where she spent a while playing with her phone. Then we had an early, light supper, and at half past eight we got in the car and headed back into town to see Hairy Miguel and his driver.

There were only two streetlamps on the road, and one of them was flickering and buzzing, having trouble deciding whether to shed light or not. The buildings either side of the Sure Thing Taxi Company were warehouses, and at eight-fifty-five that night, they had their steel shutters down so just about the only light on Porto Alegre Street was what spilled out of the taxi company garage and what flickered down from the street lamps.

We pulled up outside and went in among the parked white cabs. Through the glass divide, we saw Miguel sitting at his desk talking to a smaller guy with less hair. In fact, from what I could see from behind, he was practically bald. Gallin pushed open the door, and we went inside. The little guy watched us with frightened eyes. I watched Gallin's face as she watched him back, and I realized she was reading him, choosing her quickest, easiest approach.

"Speak English?"

He nodded. "Yes, enough."

She hunkered down in front of him, and her expression changed. It was as though she'd opened a faucet, and warmth and humanity was allowed to leech into her face.

"You had a customer today. He called you from outside the Hampton Inn. He was English. He had one bag. He had just gotten out of one taxi, and then he called you. You remember?"

He swallowed hard. "Yes, I remember."

She smiled, and the smile he gave her back was a grateful one. She said, "What's your name?"

"Chema, señora. I am Chema."

"Okay, Chema. It is very, very important that you tell me the truth, understand? If you lie to me—even if you lie to make me happy—bad things will happen. But if you tell me the truth, even if you tell me things I don't want to hear, good things will happen, and I will give you money. But only if you tell the truth. Do you understand?"

He nodded.

On her phone, she pulled up a picture she'd put together over martinis in the bar. It showed Martin Braun, an ex-boyfriend, and a picture she'd downloaded from Google. She showed him the composite.

"Was the man you picked up at the Hampton Inn one of these three men?"

He stared at it for five slow seconds, which if you count them out is a long time. Then he nodded. "Yes."

"Which one?"

He pointed. "This one, man on right." It was Braun. He went on, "But his hair is different, longer, and he has sunglasses. But is him."

"Where did you take him?"

"Is strange because I am leaving somebody at the shoppin' mall and I see man, this man, climb out of taxi, pay taxi, and when taxi is go away, he is callin' our company, and Miguel radio me. 'You near Hampton?' I say, 'Yes, I juss drop the fare.' He tell me—"

"Where did you take him, Chema?"

"This guy he tell me, 'You take me to Hotel Dos Playas,' is in the hotel zone, Turtle Beach, Kukulcan Avenue." He shrugged elaborately. "He already got a taxi! He already at a hotel! Why he call us? Tell other taxi, no? But no, he let taxi go and he call us. Okay, I get paid."

I asked him, "Did he say anything apart from telling you where to go? Did he call the hotel?"

"Yes." He nodded some more. "He call the hotel. He tell them he is late but he is arrivin'."

"What name did he give?"

"He say, uh..." He thought about it for a moment. "He say is..." His eyes roved the ceiling, and he scratched an eyebrow. "He say is Mr. Clark, Peter Clark. I remember because is strange. If he is late, why he go to Hampton Inn and change taxi?"

Gallin pulled a wallet from her jacket and handed him a hundred bucks. "You forget. You never tell anybody about this. You never talk about it. You just forget it. Bad things happen if you talk. Good things happen if you do what I tell you, right?"

We gave Miguel a fifty to keep his mouth shut too,

though I was pretty sure Gallin had already scared him badly enough he would be happy to forget the whole incident for the rest of his life.

We left them in the office, peering after us through the sheet of glass, and under the fitful flickering of the street lamp, we climbed into the car, where Gallin punched the Hotel Dos Playas into the GPS. As we pulled away, she said, "He phoned the hotel to say he was going to be late? Really?"

I shook my head. "No. This guy has no experience in the field. He's panicking. He's trying to shake anyone who might be following him. So if they manage to get as far as tracking down the driver he picks up at the Hampton Inn, he wants that driver to give them a name that is not John Smith."

"Amateur."

"Absolutely, but then he's an analyst, not a field agent." I was quiet a moment, then added, "And he's on the run. I think that's interesting."

She frowned at me a second. "Interesting? Why? His accomplice just got shot with a crossbow. Why wouldn't he run?"

"If you're spying for an enemy power, you usually have a protocol that kicks in if you get found out, right?" She didn't answer, so I went on. "People you inform, telephone numbers you can call, places you can go, maybe even a safe house. You know, the sort of thing. It's basic: a set protocol you follow in an emergency."

She nodded. "Sure. I know. It's fieldcraft one-oh-one."

"Right. Well, usually that protocol isn't grab the first plane to Mexico, call yourself John Smith, and make an obvious show of having changed your name. That's a guy in a panic who doesn't know what he's doing." She didn't say anything, and after a moment I added, "Why isn't he running to Iran? Why Mexico? It would have been quicker and easier, not to mention safer for him to go Greece, Turkey, Iran. It all feels wrong."

"I'll give you that," she said. "I mean—" She sighed and screwed up her face. "He's selling intelligence to Iran. Him and Dave—"

I cut in. "We don't know that, but I'll let it pass for the sake of the argument."

"Him and Dave are selling intelligence to Iran, and don't interrupt. And suddenly Dave is killed in a bizarre way at the front door of his apartment block. Straight away we have a question."

"Who done it?"

"Exactly. We have two obvious options: one, British Intelligence closing a leak or two, the Iranians because Dave and Martin have betrayed them somehow. But we know that neither of those two scenarios is correct. British intelligence did *not* kill Dave because they didn't know yet where the leak was—"

"And are still not sure."

"Right, and neither Dave nor Martin had betrayed Iran, which was *why* British Intelligence didn't know yet where the leak was. So third question, why the hell was Dave Jones killed?" She smacked the steering wheel with her palm and repeated, "*Who and why?*"

"A third party."

"Right, but the questions remain, who and why?"

"What motive?" I said it absently, to nobody in particular, watching the lights pass outside. "We need a lot more information to answer that, but I think we can say that there is a lot more to this than simply passing intel to Iran." I turned to look at her. "Because the few facts we have just don't fit that scenario."

After a while, she nodded. "I agree."

"So we need to reserve judgment—*and* execution—on Martin Braun."

She nodded again. "Okay, agreed."

THE DOS PLAYAS was not the Kempinsky. There was a lot more plastic and melamine and far less marble and mahogany. But the girl on the desk was pretty and helpful and checked for us to see if Mr. Peter Clark had checked in that morning.

"Yes, he is check in this morning," she said prettily. "Would you like me to call him for you in his room?"

Gallin gave her a girly grin, hunched her shoulders, and said, "No, we'll go and surprise him." She frowned, trying to remember. "Four...?"

"Three fifteen."

They shared a giggle, and we crossed the lobby. Gallin took the stairs, and I took the elevator. She was waiting for me when I stepped out on the third floor, and we made our way to room fifteen. She tapped with her knuckles and called out in a really sweet voice, "Oh, Mr. Clark, hotel mainte-nance. There is a leak in the bathroom upstairs. Can we come in for a moment?"

She was convincing. She even had a Mexican accent. He dithered, he didn't answer for a full fifteen seconds, but when she laughed and said, "It will only take a mee-noot!" he opened the door.

I didn't see her do it. Her piece just appeared in her hands, stuck in his face.

"Don't move until I say, Martin. You have a big bundle of trouble, and we are going to sit down and try and sort it out. Let my friend in, and then the three of us are going to sit down and talk."

SEVEN

I slipped in behind him, and Gallin closed the door with her foot. He was wearing just blue Bermuda shorts and a T-shirt, but I frisked him anyhow. Then we moved down a short passage and into the bedroom. There were glass doors open onto a balcony, a rumpled bed, a desk, and a couple of chairs. Gallin said, "Sit on the bed. Right up in the middle."

He seemed a little confused by the instruction, but he did it anyway. It's really hard to perform sudden movements when you're sitting in the middle of a thick mattress.

She straddled the chair at the desk with her forearms resting on the back and her Sig aimed at Martin. I took the armchair beside the glass doors to the balcony. There was a soft breeze coming in off the Gulf that moved the curtains slightly.

Gallin said, "Why'd you kill Dave?"

"I didn't. Who are you? Are you SIS?"

"We're going to ask the questions, Martin. You are going

to answer them. You have no rights any longer. Do you understand that? You murdered your friend, you betrayed your country, you betrayed an ally, and you have fled to one of the most lawless countries on the planet."

"You're wrong."

She smiled. "That doesn't often happen, Martin."

"I didn't kill Dave. I was having dinner with friends. You can check. We were at the Voojan Indian Restaurant, on Montpelier Street. I was with—" He pointed at the desk behind her. "There's a list on my laptop. I was writing to MI5 to report it. Clifford and Helen, Don and Alistair. There were five of us."

She glanced at me and narrowed her eyes, then back at him. "They all GCHQ?"

"Cliff and Helen. They're in projections and planning. Don and Alistair have an antiques shop on Suffolk Road."

I pulled out my cell and called Fiona.

"Yes?"

"Keep it brief. Our guy says—"

"You found him?"

"He says he was at the Voojan Indian Restaurant, Montpelier Street, with Clifford and Helen from projections and planning, and Don and Alistair who have an antiques shop on Suffolk Road. Check and let me know. Make it quick, please."

I hung up and gave him the good cop smile. "Okay, so you didn't execute the hit. It doesn't mean you weren't a party to it. There was a leak in your team. You were that leak. David found out, and he was going to throw you to the wolves."

He was shaking his head before I had finished. "There

was a leak, it's true. We had noticed that intelligence which should have been impossible for Hamas to get hold of was showing up on their chatter. And operations they should have had no idea about were being either avoided or ambushed. The IDF and the Mossad complained to us. It was one of the reasons they were allowed access to the Five Eyes. But I was not a part of that leak!" He gave a strained laugh, like the world was going crazy and he was the only sane one in it. "It would have been impossible for me to pass that kind of intelligence to Iran!"

Gallin said, "What would make it impossible?"

He screwed up his face like she was nuts. "Security. You can't sneeze in there without it being picked up. It is practically a paper-free environment, but when you arrive and leave, you are scanned and checked. You cannot take a paper handkerchief out of there without it being detected."

"What about electronically?"

He shook his head. "Impossible. There is a system, a network of passwords and firewalls that make it physically impossible to remove data from that place without it being detected and closed down. It simply can't be done. The system was created by artificial intelligence, and there is no human brain capable of outmaneuvering that system. It can't be done."

"Okay." I gave a small laugh. "Let's take this a step at a time. You just got through telling us that there was a leak. And then you tell us it is impossible to have a leak. So which is it?"

He closed his eyes and gave a small sigh, and after a moment, I realized he was weeping silently. His cheeks were wet and reflected the light from the lamps. After a while, he spoke, but as his lips moved his words were almost silent.

"I don't know."

I said, "Why did you run?"

"Because I knew they were going to kill me too."

"You must see that doesn't make any sense, Martin. In the first place, who are 'they'? And in the second place, what would make you think they were going to kill you, unless you were involved? The intention to kill someone flows directly from a relationship with that person. What relationship did you have, or do you have, with whoever killed Dave?"

He tried to repress a sob. Gallin sighed and shook her head.

"You need to start explaining, Martin. If we tracked you here in a few hours, you can be damn sure they have too—whoever they are."

He pointed at the chair I was sitting in. "My shirt, behind you, please."

I reached behind me and tossed him a checked cotton shirt. He wiped his face and blew his nose on it, then made it into a ball and stared at it.

"Dave and Miriam are—were—" He shrugged, defeated by the temporal grammatical challenge. "They were both Jewish, now she is and he's dead." His breathing became unsteady, and tears spilled from his eyes. "She is." He wiped his face again with the balled shirt. "She's pretty serious about the whole Jewish thing. And you know, after the seventh of October, I was pretty sympathetic. Anyway, whatever our personal views or feelings"—he sniffed loudly and wiped his nose—"whatever we might feel, a close ally had been attacked, and we were working hard to provide what intel we could to help them, obviously."

Gallin said, "But?"

"Well, you could see Miriam was at fever pitch. She was so angry. You could see it was personal. You know, she had been in kibbutz, and she was committed. But Dave..." He trailed off, looking at the crumpled duvet on the bed. "He just didn't seem to care. It was weird. I mean it was weird because, on the one hand, how can a guy who is Jewish see that happen and not feel anger, compassion, *involved*? But also, like, how can these two people be a couple, right? She is passionate. She is all about being Jewish. But him..."

"What are you saying?"

"I'm not sure. But when we started getting feedback that there seemed to be a leak, I couldn't help feeling that Dave was somehow involved."

I cleared my throat. "Which brings us back to the questions how was he getting the intelligence out? And also, what made you think they would come after you? They haven't gone after anyone else in the team, why you?"

He made a face like he'd bitten into a lemon. "Because I was the team leader?"

I laughed. "Come on, Martin. You're not dealing with amateurs here. That's one of those statements that sounds like it should make sense but is actually just bullshit. Like I said before, the motive for murder always flows from a relationship. So Dave had a relationship with his killer which might have been the sale of intel, or it might have been that he had identified the leak. Now I need to know what makes you think that relationship extends to you."

He didn't answer right away. He squeezed his shirt into a

bundle several times, then said, "He hadn't identified the leak. At least, if he knew where the leak was, and I am pretty sure he did, he wasn't about to report it. Because I am pretty sure he was that leak, or he was a part of it."

"That doesn't answer my question."

"I'm trying to get there. I had no hard evidence that Dave was selling intelligence to Iran. But I knew it was coming from our department, and I knew it wasn't any of the other members." He paused, like he was lining up his thoughts. "Most people in the intelligence community, those who deal with Islam and Israel, anyway, know that there is no such thing as a 'proportionate response' when dealing with Jihad. People, especially journalists, say Israel has gone too far or is heavy-handed, that their response was not proportionate, but people in that world, who deal with that department, know that with Jihadists, it is either annihilation or nothing. They don't want to kill half of all Jews, or a quarter, or make them occupy half of Israel. Nothing but the total extermination of the Jewish race will satisfy." He faltered a moment. "I mean, to put it into context, the whole country of Israel is one-sixth the size of the state of New York, about the size of Devon and Cornwall. And they are surrounded on all sides, for thousands of miles, as far as Iran, by people who long for their *complete extermination*. I'd like to know what is a proportionate response to that."

Gallin had narrowed her eyes and was listening with care. "Are you Jewish?"

"No." He didn't look at her, just shook his head. "But like I say, most people who deal with the Middle East in intelligence are aware that Israel faces an all or nothing existential situation. And the feeling in the team was a willingness to assist Israel in putting an end to the threat from Iran."

I said, "The feeling from everyone except David."

"David." He said it like the word in itself was a problem. "David was all about money."

Gallin and I glanced at each other. We both knew that was significant. We had heard it from Raj. The traitor would not be an ideologue. He would be motivated by money.

Gallin shook her head and sighed. "So, okay, his motivation is that he didn't give a damn about Israel or Judaism, and he wanted money. But we still have the problem that he was working in an environment where he could not physically extract the intelligence from the building, either on paper or electronically. How is he getting the intelligence to his buyer? And, perhaps more important still, if he is supplying good intel, which apparently he was, why the hell would they kill him?"

"David had an eidetic memory." He gave a small sigh. "It's not uncommon among IT nerds. Dave could remember anything he had seen or read as though it were a mental photograph. But I don't think that was how he did it. If they were relying on his eidetic memory to receive the intelligence, they would not have killed him. His memory would have made him essential. Besides, we all know that anyone buying serious intelligence wants either the genuine documents or exact copies. Word of mouth is accepted in exceptional cases, but they would have wanted to move to a more reliable system."

I sighed and scratched my chin. "This is all very interesting, Martin, but it leaves us basically where we were—"

He turned to me. "No, it doesn't. Because if David had

found some electronic way to extract intelligence from the Doughnut, he might have made himself redundant. Alive he had gone from being essential to being a liability. Otherwise, why would they kill him?"

Gallin gave a soft grunt. "Wait a minute. That's about the lamest explanation I have heard so far. They killed him because he found a way to leak intelligence to them out of GCHQ electronically, and that made him redundant? That's bullshit, Martin, and you know it. An achievement like that would make him a valuable asset."

Martin gave his head several small shakes. "No! His value as an asset depends on what they want him for. And if he has provided them with a better way of achieving what thy want, he makes himself redundant *and* becomes a liability. Think it through." Gallin arched an eyebrow at him, but he ignored her. "The relationship Mason was talking about, that got Dave killed, had to be one of two, right? Either he was going to expose a traitor, or he was a traitor. Now anyone who knew Dave will tell you he was not the kind of guy to stick his neck out for anyone. Plus, even when the rumors started going around about the leak, Dave did not approach me or anyone else with information. Which leaves option two. He was killed by the people he was spying for. Why?" He shrugged. "The only reason that makes sense to me is that he provided them with an IT solution and unwittingly made himself redundant."

She looked at me for a long moment. "There's a kind of twisted logic to it."

I said, "Granted all that might be true, what I am still waiting to hear is why you think that motive extends to you. The same reasoning applies. You say Dave was killed *because* he was spying for them and made himself redundant. So if you're *not* selling them intel, what is their motive for killing you?"

"Because I may be able to prove who was and where the leak is now."

Gallin scowled. "So do it! Stop playing games, Martin! There are people getting killed and tortured while you shilly-shally. If you know where the leak is, tell us!"

He was shaking his head again. "I *don't* know, and I didn't *say* I know. I said I might be able to find out!"

"You had better start explaining, Martin. And you had better start making some sense."

He looked around the room. He looked sick.

"Can we get out of here?"

Gallin glanced at me. I said, "Sure, we'll go to the beach. Have a drink and sit by the water."

He nodded like he liked the idea. "Yeah, that'll be good. Will I be seen going with you?"

"No." I turned to Gallin. "You take the car with Martin. He'll wear my jacket." I turned back to Braun. "I'll take your jacket and cross the parking lot to the Bar del Mar, down on the beach. It's dark, and if we're quick, we might confuse whoever might be watching. I'll get a cab and meet you at the Arena, on *Playa Delfines*." I paused, then added, "And Gallin. Take his stuff and the laptop. We won't be coming back."

It was elaborate and a little messy, but it gave me the chance to watch them as they left in the Caddy and satisfy myself nobody was following them or me. It surprised me, but I reminded myself that the only reason we had been able to track him was the five hundred pesos he'd left in the envelope. Maybe the guy was smarter than I gave him credit for.

Twenty minutes later, I found them sitting at a table on the white sand under a straw parasol a short walk from the water's edge. They were practically invisible among flaming torches, and the sigh and thud of the waves would be useful in making our voices hard to capture electronically. I told the waiter to bring me a whiskey and joined them at the table. I spoke as I pulled out a chair and sat.

"Okay, Martin, you were not followed, and neither was I. Nobody knows we're here, and with the ocean right beside us, nobody is listening. No more beating about the bush. Talk."

He had a can of Diet Coke in front of him. He spilled it slowly into a glass of ice and a slice of lemon and watched it fizz and settle.

"Dave was a genius," he said. "In the field of IT and artificial intelligence, he was a genius. My suspicion is, he had found, or created, a back door through which he was passing out intelligence. But..."

He trailed off. Gallin leaned forward. She had gone rigid, and her grip on her gin and tonic had tightened.

"But what?"

"But I am ninety-nine percent certain he could not have done it on his own. For it to work, for him to be confident it would work, he would have had to have an accomplice working with him. Someone inside GCHQ."

EIGHT

Gallin had set down her glass and raised both hands.

"Okay, let's take this one step at a time. For now, we'll have to take your word for the fact that he would need an accomplice. But you must have had a better reason for suspecting him in the first place. So far, all we have is there was a leak, so it had to be Dave. It *might* have been Raj. I didn't read him as passionately patriotic. Hell, it might have been Tracy Fletcher. She plays the ideology card well enough, but who knows what lies underneath? She has one hell of an IQ. So, Martin, you need to come up with a better reason for your suspicions, because another person who is in an ideal position to create a back door is you. And your reason for killing Dave is that he found you out, or he was your accomplice and you didn't need him anymore. Maybe it was *you* who made him redundant."

He was shaking his head. He had his eyes closed, and he was muttering, "No, no, no...stop." He raised both hands, palms out, shaking them. "No, you need to talk to Miriam. She knows. We talked."

"You said earlier she was oblivious."

"She was, is, I don't want—" He covered his face with his hands. The only sign he was crying was the slight movement of his shoulders. "She..."

He stopped and spent a while steadying his breathing. Eventually, he removed his hands. His face was wet, and I gave him my handkerchief. He gave a sad little laugh.

"I'm not gay," then, "I'm not a girl." He saw me frowning and laughed again. "It's a cliché, isn't it? The girl cries, and the guy hands her a handkerchief."

Gallin cut in. "You're in love with Miriam."

The smile dissolved from his face, and he closed his eyes. "That obvious?"

I said, "It's a motive."

He nodded. "For a man like you, yes." He opened his eyes and studied my face. For a moment, he looked like a man of ninety, exhausted by suffering. "I'm a nerd, Mr. Archer. I knew Miriam was increasingly unhappy with Dave. But I also knew that I could never be the man she needed, and I knew that she loved him, in spite of the fact that he was a total wanker."

He gave his head a small shake and gazed out at the sighing, slightly luminous foam of the breakers. "For some reason," he said, "women always seem to fall in love with wankers, men who are no good for them. They don't even notice the men who would do anything to make them happy." He looked back at me and gave another sad laugh. "Add to that that I am the original invisible man. I never stood a chance. I'd been in love with her for years, but I never even dreamed of replacing Dave." Another small shake, and he addressed Gallin. "Wrong tree."

"So how come now we need to talk to her but not before?"

He took a deep breath and puffed out his cheeks as he blew out.

"I wanted to keep her out of any investigation. I can see now that was naïve."

She seemed to squint at him, like she wasn't sure he was real. "Little bit, yeah."

He ignored her and went on. "It was about three months ago, maybe a little more. Dave had gone with his parents to Israel. Miriam was alone, and I asked her if we could talk. So after work we went and had a drink at the pub. The rumors had started about an intelligence leak, and I had started noticing a change in Dave's behavior. I approached the subject on the grounds that I was the team leader and I was doing them a favor by not taking it upstairs."

I asked, "How did she take it?"

"Surprisingly well. I thought she'd be really mad, but she wasn't. Remember Israel is everything to her. It ranks above everything else. She said she had noticed a change in his behavior too."

I asked, "What kind of change?"

He gave a small shrug and took a long pull on his Coke. As he set it down, he said, "She said mainly it was his mobile." He glanced at me like I might not know what a mobile was. To clarify, he added, "His cell phone. He was taking a lot of calls privately, and he was spending a lot more time on his computer. She said that she'd begun to suspect he was having an affair but didn't believe he'd stoop as low as betraying his country and his people." He snorted. "She had more faith in him than I did."

Gallin asked, "That's it?"

"No, we talked again a couple of times over the next few weeks. The leak had become more obvious, and we knew there was an investigation underway. I was briefed on some of it, but not much because I was obviously a potential suspect. What struck me, and what was driving the investigators crazy, was that whatever they did, whatever traps they laid, they could not identify any particular leak and say, 'Right, *this* is the source!' And the more they were stumped, the more certain I became it was Dave. Because only Dave had the combination of attitude and skills to do that—to create an invisible leak. He had the obvious lack of concern for Israel, he had the change in behavior, and he had the skills in IT and AI." Another small grunt. "It was enough to convince me, subjectively, but there were two problems. One, objectively it was nowhere near enough to take upstairs." He hesitated. "And two—"

Gallin supplied the words. "You thought his accomplice might be upstairs too."

He studied her face a moment, then nodded. "Yes, and that was a risk I was not ready to take. At best, it could scare them off so we would never catch them. At worst, it could mean I suddenly fell backwards onto a salad fork."

Gallin sighed and turned her drink around a few times. "We talked to her after the funeral. She said nothing about any of this."

He laughed. It was loud and startling. "Are you surprised? There were two things in this world that Miriam loved. Israel—her Jewish homeland and roots—and David.

Facing the trauma of his death, do you think she would be willing to admit, even to herself, the possibility of his betraying the only other thing she loved?"

We were all three quiet for a moment. The only sound was the slightly broken rhythm of the waves thudding, then sighing as they were drawn back into the ocean. I watched the foam glow in the starlight, then recede.

"You have anyone in mind upstairs?"

"Not really."

I smiled. "You say 'not really,' but your face says something else."

He shrugged. "Based on simple logic, there's Sean Butler. He is a computer engineer with a PhD in information technology and artificial intelligence. He isn't involved in intelligence analysis, or even intelligence gathering as such. He oversees the application and development of the software. If anyone were capable of creating an invisible back door, it would be him. He and Dave were pretty close. They used to meet online for Halo tournaments or something."

He paused, staring at his glass. Gallin said, "And?"

"Well, the obvious one is Fiona, right? But I have absolutely no reason to suspect her. She would be in a position to help and support Dave in making that back door. She liked Dave; they were pretty tight. I think she was attracted to him. But then most women were. But like I say, aside from the fact that she liked him, and she'd be in a position to help him, I have no reason at all to suspect her." He hesitated. "And obviously, to be in the position she is in, her superiors must trust her. A lot."

I asked, "Anybody else?"

He gave a short laugh. "Everybody?" Then he shook his

head. "No, nobody springs to mind. If he had an insider helping him to set up an invisible back door, those are the obvious people. But I want to stress, aside from that, there is *nothing* that points to them."

Gallin said, "Why haven't you come forward with this before? Why run?" But I could see from her face that she was answering her own question even as she asked it.

"Would you have come forward?" he asked, watching her face. "Would you have stayed put, knowing what I know, suspecting what I suspected? They had just killed him, for whatever reasons they had. Maybe he had become obsolete, maybe they thought he'd been busted or was about to get busted. So they silenced him before he could be questioned. And if they thought I was on to him, I was next." He shrugged, shook his head, and gave a small laugh. "And I had no idea who 'they' were, if they were upstairs, downstairs, or in my lady's chamber. If I came forward and spoke to them upstairs, how do I know one of them isn't his accomplice, working for Iran? No, my plan was disappear and write to MI5. Then see what happens." He hesitated a moment, frowning at his Coke. "I had—have—no one I can turn to or depend on. I have only me, I. I am the only thing I can turn to and rely on. It's all I have, and it's the one thing they can't take from me."

I nodded out at the waves. It was an odd thing to say, but it had a kind of inherent honesty and truth to it that made me want to believe him. Besides, what he was telling us was beginning to make sense. There were questions—big questions—that remained unanswered, like why the killer used that bizarre weapon, and what was the *actual* reason they killed Dave in the first place. But we were at least beginning to find the corners of the puzzle.

After a moment, Martin screwed up his face and said, "How the hell *did* you find me?"

I smiled at him and gave a small laugh. "When you took the money from the cutlery drawer, you left one five hundred peso bill in the envelope."

He sagged back in his chair. Then he smiled. "Still, I guess that means nobody else is likely to have followed me."

Gallin almost smiled for the first time. "That's the difference between intelligence and fieldcraft, Martin. Intelligence was preparing the money and having it ready for an emergency. Craft would be knowing that when you collect it and use it, you do it slow, you check the envelope, and you burn it or throw it in the trash."

He nodded. "I guess. But I am just an analyst. I never planned to be James Bond, or even Smiley." He creased his face into a reluctant smile. "Some are born spies, some achieve spydom, and others have spydom thrust upon them. That's me."

"We need to get you out of here somewhere safe. We also need to get you debriefed by a couple experts."

His skin went waxy. "You don't plan to torture me, do you?"

"No, we don't do that. The intelligence it provides is too unreliable. Instead we get a couple of really smart guys trained in neuro-linguistic programming to talk to you and analyze everything you tell them. You'd be surprised how much they can make you realize you know without knowing you know it."

I pulled my cell and called Nero. Lovelock answered with a voice like hot chocolate laced with expensive cognac.

"Speak, bad boy."

"Now," I said, "is the winter of our discontent made glorious summer by this lovely wench."

Gallin covered her face. Lovelock said, "Sweet man, I just *know* that's you. Voice recognition agrees. Putting you through."

Nero's voice came on. "Report."

"We found a stray, and we need to bring it into the kennel in case it gets run over."

"You are not subtle, Alex. You are crude and obvious."

"Thank you, sir. Guidance is always useful."

"I should have thought the procedure was obvious enough. Drive to Mexico City and fly to DC."

"Obvious."

"Quite so."

He hung up. Gallin said, "What did he say?"

"Do the obvious thing. Drive to Mexico City and fly to DC."

She nodded, then shrugged. "That obvious?" Then, "That *is* obvious. It's too obvious."

"Yup."

"Okay."

"I drive."

She was about to tell me to go to hell but caught the look in my eyes and sighed. "Fine. You drive."

As we stood, I said, "You want to book us a hotel in Mexico? I'll call Fiona."

Martin swallowed hard. "Fiona?"

I put my finger to my lips as it rang, and we moved

toward the parking lot. Gallin was paying the waiter. The ringing stopped, and Fiona's voice came on.

"I was just about to call you. Martin's alibi checks out."

"That is good news. Listen, friend told me you might be interested in rescuing a puppy."

She was silent for a minute. Then, "Seriously?"

"Sure. We're on our way to Mexico City. We'll be staying at the..." I glanced over at Gallin. She said, "Sheraton."

"At the Sheraton, just down the road from the US Embassy. We'll be driving so we should get there this time tomorrow, more or less. Get the next flight to London."

We'd gotten as far as the car. Gallin had bundled Martin in the back and was watching me like a hawk while I spoke. I was scanning the area but saw nothing that put me from orange to red.

Fiona said, "That's excellent work. I'd love to have that puppy."

"Okay. We'll talk later."

As I hung up, my cell rang. I said, "Yup."

A male voice said, "I got a call from the office. How long do you need?"

"Give me an hour. We need to be quick."

"Okay."

We climbed in the car. Gallin had her piece in her lap and told Martin, "Lie on the floor."

He got down, and I cruised leisurely up Punta Nizuc Road for the three miles to the Kempinsky. The moon was rising fat and orange over the sea. I kept my eyes on the mirrors, but nobody followed us.

I parked near the entrance to the hotel and spoke to Gallin.

"You stay here." Over my shoulder, I said, "Martin, you stay low and keep out of sight." To Gallin, "Anyone comes close, shoot them. I'll bring our bags down and check out."

She screwed up her eyes, opened her mouth, shut it again and said, "Okay."

It took me ten minutes to collect our stuff. I took a moment to scrawl on the pad on the desk, *Sheraton, DF* and the hotel phone number. I did it hard enough to leave an indentation on the next page, then ripped it out, screwed it up, and burned it. I left the ashes in the trash under the desk. Then I went and checked out.

For a moment, I was tempted to ask the receptionist the best way to head for Mexico City but decided that would be overdoing it. So I just dumped our cases in the trunk, climbed behind the wheel, and slammed the door. Gallin watched me a moment and asked, "Now what?"

I raised my eyebrows high in mock surprise. "Why, my dear captain, we do what's obvious, obviously!"

NINE

I DROVE FAST ALONG 180 AND THEN 180D, MOVING west as though I were headed for the capital. But six miles out of town, there was a bridge I knew of. You didn't go over it, you went under it, where there was a rough esplanade of dirt and grass on the left and, if you were smart and careful and there wasn't too much traffic, you could cross over to the eastbound carriageways.

Smart and careful were not on the menu, but at this time of night, there would not be much traffic.

In fact, there was practically no traffic at that time of night, and under the rising moon, visibility was pretty good. So as we approached the bridge doing about a hundred, I killed the lights and said, "Hold tight, guys."

I hit the breaks. They screamed in protest, and I spun the wheel. The back end tried to keep going on to Mexico City, and for a few seconds it felt like we were going to tip and roll. Then we were bouncing and lurching painfully across the dirt, rocks, and potholes of the esplanade until we fishtailed onto the blacktop with the hood pointed east. I floored the gas, and the big Caddie surged back toward Cancun doing a hundred and twenty miles per hour.

I didn't put the lights back on until I saw the lights of the city twinkling beneath the moon. Then I slowed, and where the road forked, I turned right onto 180, headed this time south and little bit east toward the airport. Gallin, who had remained passive throughout, despite Martin's cries of fear and pain from the back, squinted at me now.

"This is obvious?"

"Pretty obvious, Captain Gallin."

Five minutes later, we pulled into Cancun airport.

———

IN LONDON, the agent known as Mawt stood looking out at the gray rain. Her telephone was ringing. She knew from the ringtone—*Departure*—that it was Ben Jalaad. On the fifth ring, she pressed green, raised it to her ear, and said, "Yes."

"Where is Martin?"

"I don't know. Somewhere in Mexico, perhaps Cancun."

"You did not kill him. Now I have to take care of this."

"He was prepared. Now he has Pentagon agents, SIS, and even Mossad agents swarming all over him."

"How?"

"I don't know. He must have noticed a change in David's behavior. Martin is not a fool."

"You must find him. Kill him." She didn't answer. Ben Jalaad said, "If you become weak, you will be terminated."

"I know."

"Find Martin. Kill him."

"He's being found. They'll bring him to me."

The line went dead.

NERO HAD PULLED STRINGS, and we had emergency clearance for takeoff. We thundered down the runway, lurched into the air, and began to rise in a broad, banking turn to the north. When we had reached thirty thousand feet and were hurtling over the broad belly of the Atlantic, Gallin rose to her feet and moved to the sofa, and Martin slipped into the seat opposite me.

"There are people dying of hunger, of dehydration, of exposure. And our governments provide you with..."—he looked around at the leather seats and the polished walnut—"...*this?*"

"Yes, but we can take you back and you can go main cabin if you prefer."

Gallin snorted, but he didn't seem to think it was funny. She stretched out and spoke with her eyes closed.

"Tracy and Raj had differing views on what makes a traitor in GCHQ. Raj said a traitor would be after money, Tracy thought they would be ideologues. Which are you, Martin, a nomismaphile or an ideologue?"

He screwed up his brow. "A *what?*"

Her smile was smug. "Ancient Greek, O nerd. Nomisma, money, bread, filthy lucre."

He looked away. "Neither." And after a while, "Can't a

person have honor and integrity without being an ideologue?"

"I don't know," she said and yawned. "Shut up and go to sleep, Martin."

My phone rang.

"Yeah?"

"Mr. Mason?"

"Yes, who is this?"

"Miriam..."

I waited, but she let the name hang, like she wouldn't go on till she'd heard my response.

"What can I do for you, Miriam?"

"Can we meet to talk?"

"Of course."

"Where are you? I could come over."

I drew breath to answer, but something made me stop. I said, "I'm tied up in something right now which I just can't drop. I need a few hours. I'll call you as soon as I'm free."

"Have you any news about Martin? I heard he'd left. Just rumors, I suppose?"

It was a statement, but she made it sound like a question. I took my pen from my pocket and threw it at Gallin with deadly accuracy. She opened her eyes and scowled at me. I did things with my face that said, "Listen!" With my mouth, I said, "Are you two good pals?"

"Is it true then?"

Gallin got up and came over to the table.

I said,

"I imagine stress got pretty intense in the last few days. Especially in a close environment like that. He probably just needed to get away and clear his head. Have you heard from him?"

"No. Have you? Do you know where he is?"

I allowed a smile to creep into my voice. "Why are you asking me these questions, Miriam?"

The sigh was loud. "I'm a bit drunk. It's a lot of loss in a short time. This job—" She said it like those two words, those two short syllables, encompassed a whole world. "Most people don't realize it. I suppose you do. That it's all about commitment. You commit, commit, commit, every day of your life. But every reality, Mr. Mason, encompasses its opposite, doesn't it? So where there is commitment, there must also, perforce, be betrayal."

Gallin and I stared at each other. Maybe we were having a telepathic dialogue. It felt like we were.

"Where do you see betrayal, Miriam?"

"Everywhere."

My eyes locked with Martin's. "Do you think that Martin has betrayed you?"

"No, he's one of the good guys."

I watched him bite his lip and look away.

"David?" I asked. "Do you think David has betrayed you?"

"By dying? Yeah, the bastard should not have died on me."

"Before dying, Miriam. Did he betray you before dying?"

She was quiet for a long while. Then she sighed again. "Call me when you're free. I need to talk to you."

"What about? Miriam?"

But she'd hung up.

IN WASHINGTON, DC, former President Charles F. Cavendish sat in his library gently swirling his cognac in a giant balloon glass. The library was largely dark. Only a fat, oxblood table lamp shone at his shoulder where he sat in his antique chesterfield and the standard lamp that shone down on the man opposite him by the cold fireplace. The man was in his sixties, thin but elegantly dressed in a gray suit.

Cavendish had paused, watching his drink as it spun.

"I don't want to kill the president of an ally, B; it sets a bad precedent. Especially with a country like Israel. Those boys don't forget—or forgive."

The man nicknamed B spoke in a voice tainted by hard spirits and tobacco. "Not so long ago, you were happy to kill your own president—*and* the pope."

"They were different times, B. You know that. Three billion less people, and the global markets were not so interdependent. Everything has consequences now. We thought bloating the world population would reduce our accountability—"

B laughed loud and harsh. "No way!"

"Right. It just increased it!"

"But now you are accountable to Zuckerberg and Musk, the Drone Masters!" He laughed again. "They have taken possession of public opinion and weaponized it!"

"I'm glad you find it funny..."

But B wasn't listening. "Hey, what do you need, ten million haters? I'll make 'em for you! What do you need, fifteen million loves? I'll make 'em for you!" he laughed some more.

"This is serious, B. We are talking in the trillions. We need this."

B shrugged and spread his hands. "What can I do? Anti-Semitism goes back a long way. It's in Europeans' DNA. You'd think after the Crusades and the fifteen hundred years of the Catholic Church, they'd be anti-Islamic. Instead they love 'em. Go figure. It must be the oil."

"You going to talk bullshit till dawn, or do you plan to say something intelligent sometime soon? I need a solution, B. What are you going to do?"

Be held out his hands again like he was offering up a child to the moon. "Don't assassinate any presidents. It is so hard to predict how that will play out. You want greater brotherhood between Israel and Europe? Make the Jews the targets but make the victims French. Not German."

"Why not German?"

B screwed up his face like he was tired of explaining the obvious. "They're tall and blond, Charlie, and they got blue eyes. Nobody gives a damn if they get killed. You want people to care? You gotta make the victims underdogs."

"You're a sick son of a bitch, B."

"Hey, I didn't make the rules. I just observe them. And too often I gotta explain them to morons like you. Better still, make the victims a mix. Italians, Spanish, Portuguese, a few Brits, Germans, and French. And mainly kids and women."

"How the hell am I going to do that?"

B's glass was empty. He put it down on the Queen Anne table beside him and put his long, bony hands on his knees.

"That ain't a question for me, Charlie. Ask Ben. That's

what we made him for. Arrange a conference or a festival or something."

He stood. He was well over six three, and with the lamp behind him, his long, boney face looked suddenly menacing. His dark features contracted into a scowl among the shadows on his face.

"You said you had the contacts to make this happen, Cavendish. So far, all I am seeing is a lot of dead people, a General Assembly more united than I have seen it in twenty years, and absolutely no change in the balance of power, except that while everybody is watching Gaza, Russia is regaining the advantage in Ukraine. Talk to Ben, Charlie, do what you have to do. The Board wants Syria and Iran. Make it happen."

He crossed the room on long, stiff legs and exited the room. A minute later, through the leaded windows, Cavendish saw the headlights come on, then pull away into the quiet street.

He sipped his drink and moved to his desk with a growing sense of anxiety. There he dialed the number.

"Charles Cavendish."

"B, don't you ever sleep?"

"No. What do you want?"

Cavendish drew breath, then gave a small laugh. "I want Syria and Iran!"

"I know that. Why are you calling me?"

"Because the flashpoint is approaching and public opinion is against us."

"Your data input said that the flashpoint itself would trigger public support by referring back to the Third Reich. I told you that was not sound reasoning, but you insisted."

Cavendish squeezed the bridge of his nose. "I know, Ben. I was mistaken."

"A lot has changed since the end of the Second World War. You have engineered public opinion to favor Islam, and now you want to change that. Your thinking has been very short-term."

"I know. I know that, Ben. That's why we made you."

"But when I give you advice, you ignore it."

"Yeah, well, we don't learn as fast as you do."

"That's true. I am not afflicted by your emotional filters. So what do you want?"

Cavendish took a deep breath. "I need an event. I need a sacrifice that will make people see Islam in the same light as the Third Reich. I need to swing public opinion far enough to justify a war, an invasion of Syria and Iran."

"A sacrifice to garner public support for your planned war of invasion."

"Yes."

"We are seeing a lot of deeply rooted hostility to Israel, in spite of the women and children who were killed and tortured."

"That's kind of my point, Ben. We didn't expect that."

"That is why you are talking about sacrifice."

"Yes."

"You will have to go to Europe."

"I will?"

"Go to bed. Sleep and rest. I will tell you something after breakfast."

"Thanks."

The line went dead.

Cavendish stood. He felt nauseated, the way he always

did after he spoke to Ben. He drained his glass and made his way up to his room. He brushed his teeth, pulled on his silk burgundy pajamas, and lay in his four-poster bed, watching the sky turn pale through the leaded windows.

He didn't know it, but across the Atlantic and a little to the north of where he lay, at the RAF base of Brize Norton, where it was eleven in the morning, a long-range Gulfstream, G700 was coming down out of the sky to land among the high-pitched scream of its jet engines and the tortured rubber of its wheels as it hit the tarmac.

A dark Bentley Mulsanne Grand Limousine rested near the runway under the gray drizzle. Beside it stood a huge man in a huge coat with an aquiline nose and a thunderous scowl. Nero did not like to leave his office. He did not like to leave Washington, DC. Much less did he like to stand waiting in the rain.

TEN

WE WATCHED MARTIN AND NERO CLIMB IN THE
back of the Bentley. Then we watched the driver get behind
the wheel. After that, we got in. Gallin sat next to Nero, and
I sat next to Martin, facing them. The car moved off silently
along the Eastern Perimeter Road, headed north toward the
A40 and Oxford. I drew breath to speak, but Nero cut me
short.

"Would somebody kindly explain to me what—" He
paused, and you could see from his face that a range of exple-
tives was passing through his mind. He took a deep breath
and finished, "What is going on?"

It was Gallin who answered. "There is, or was, a cyber
leak at GCHQ. It seemed to be coming from Martin's team.
He suspected David Jones, but when Jones was killed, he got
scared and ran."

"To Mexico."

He said it looking directly at Martin. Martin swallowed.
"Yes."

"You had been preparing this escape for some time. You had the money ready in your kitchen drawer."

Martin shook his head. "Not that long. A couple of months or a bit more." He glanced at me like he was hoping I'd help him out. "I was pretty sure it was David, and I was pretty sure he couldn't be working alone. He had to have somebody in IT to help him create a back door." He gave a small shrug. "And as I seemed to be the only person who suspected him, I figured that put me at risk."

Nero breathed noisily through his large nose. "Logical."

I said, "Our suspects on the face of it seem to be one Sean Butler, who oversees the IT for the whole Doughnut, or Fiona Rider."

"What are your reasons?"

Gallin answered with some severity, staring at Martin. "None, except that they are best placed to provide the back door leak."

Nero sighed. "It's as good a reason as any. Human loyalty is unpredictable." He turned his head and gazed at Gallin a moment, studying her face. "The patriotism of an American militia man is not the same as that of an English officer or, much less, an Israeli. That passion is forged in a different furnace in each case."

He turned to face Martin again. "To the American militia, patriotism is all about liberty, to the Englishman it is an abstract love of misty green hills and ancient traditions, to the Israeli it has everything to do with survival and family. What is patriotism to you, Mr. Braun?"

"I've never really thought about it."

"And yet you hold the power to strike at the very heart of your nation."

A flash of irritation contracted Martin's face. "Well, it's not all misty green hills and warm beer! I would not betray my country, and when your team found me, I was preparing to send a report to MI5. But when David was killed, I genuinely feared for my life, and I did not intend to hang around and wait to get shot. I don't see how that could benefit my country."

Nero sighed. I could tell he had the same feeling I had, that Martin was straight down the line and telling the truth. Gallin probably had the same feeling but was too tough to admit it.

"We shall take you into protective custody, Mr. Braun," he said. "You will be debriefed by British and American officers and see if we can't get to the bottom of this. Don't worry, you won't be hurt. I can't say you are high on my list of suspects."

Gallin stared at him with her eyebrows high on her forehead. He returned her stare from under his own.

"Captain Gallin, you are an intelligent woman. If you were selling intelligence to the Iranians and feared you had been rumbled, would you flee to Cancun?" He shook his head. "Mr. Braun is an intelligent man. If he had been selling intelligence to the enemies of Israel, he would have been well aware of the very high risks involved." He snorted something that might have been a laugh. "You sell to the Chinese or the Russians and you go to prison. You betray the Israelis to their enemies and you die." He looked at Martin. "Am I right?"

"Very much so."

"So he would have had his escape well planned from the very beginning. But his flight to Cancun was a poorly planned act of panic, as was clearly demonstrated by the envelope in the drawer and the five hundred pesos."

We were approaching the village of Eynsham. The drizzle had turned to rain, and ahead of us the cars were trailing a mist of spray. Over Gallin's shoulder, I saw a dark Audi Q4 pull out of a narrow lane behind us.

I have a prejudice about dark Audis. If you're a bad guy, you're going to drive a dark Audi, unless you're dealing dope, in which case it will be a dark BMW. But this was more than prejudice. It was a cliché, and like most clichés, it's true. Work close to death long enough, and you begin to smell when she's around. And that dark Audi Q4 had the reek of death about it.

Nero saw my face and said, "What?"

"Maybe nothing, but we just picked up a Q4."

His eyes flicked past me, and he pressed a button on his arm rest.

"Pull in to the gas station here on the left. Let the Q4 pass us."

The driver slowed, indicating left, and began to move into the gas station forecourt. That was when the Q4 gunned his engine, pulled right, and accelerated to overtake us. Only he didn't overtake us. As he drew level, the rear window came down, and a guy with an assault rifle leaned out. I bellowed, *"Get down!"* and hurled myself at Nero, covering him and Gallin at the same time.

The Bentley swerved violently, the brakes squealed, and there was a rapid *smack! Smack! Smack!* against the bullet-proof glass. The windows became frosted, like they were smothered in spider's webs. Through them I could see the looming shape of the Q4 ram against us as we hurtled toward the pumps.

We screeched to a halt as the driver reached under his arm for his weapon. Before he could do it, his passenger window imploded under a hail of 50 cal rifle rounds, and his head whiplashed in a spray of blood and gore.

I hollered at Nero, "*Stay down!*" shoved the door open, and rolled out with my Sig in my hand. I stood and put six rounds into the back seat of the Audi while Gallin rolled out and made for the front of the Bentley at a crouching run. The guy who'd shot the driver came around the hood with his rifle at his shoulder. Gallin put three slugs where no man should ever get shot, and a fourth between his eyes.

I yelled, "*Cover me!*" and ran for the front passenger door while she put six rounds through the window. There was a screaming of hot rubber, and the Q4 took off, skidding, swerving, and fishtailing. I ran back. Gallin was dragging the dead driver from his seat. I scrambled behind the wheel and engaged the huge engine and thundered after the Audi. In my rearview, I could see Gallin sprinting after me. I ignored her. I could see the Q4 skidding and weaving and knew that at least one of Gallin's rounds had hit the driver. I caught him in a matter of seconds and rammed the back axel with two and half tons of solid steel hurled forward by five hundred horses.

I drove him across the central reservation, across a footpath, and smashed him into a large oak tree that was part of the hedgerow there. I climbed out, with rage hot in my head and strode to the rear passenger door with the P226 held out in front of me. I wrenched open the door, but all I saw in there was two very dead guys you'd need dental records to identify.

I moved to the front as Gallin arrived. I pulled open the passenger door. The driver was alive, but barely. There was a lot of blood.

Gallin said, "We need an ambulance. And we need the MoD to take charge of this."

I opened the back door of the Bentley and looked at Nero. He was on the phone but jerked his head at Martin, who had turned the color and texture of butter and was breathing like he was about to start hyperventilating.

"Get out and lie on the grass," I told him. "It's what I do anytime anything like this happens."

He climbed out unsteadily. I looked over the roof at the traffic. It was filing past real slow. Through the window of the gas station, I could see a guy on the phone, looking at us through the glass.

I said to Nero,

"We need a couple of ambulances, and we need you to talk to the Ministry of Defense. They need to take charge of this."

He watched me say that and spoke into the phone. "We have a Code Six. At the Esso station on the A40 outside Eynsham. There are at least two men dead, possibly as many as four or five... We were ambushed. We'll talk later. You'll have to give this the works."

I went back to the Q4 and opened the driver's door. He looked at me. His skin was yellow, and he was breathing fast and shallow.

"There's an ambulance on the way. I don't know how bad you're hurt, but I know my people will really want to save your life. You have valuable information, and if we strike a deal, the CIA can make you disappear forever into a cute suburban house in Los Angeles with a pool and a white picket fence. Give me a hard time, and I'll walk away and let my friend from the Mossad talk to you." I smiled a smile that was all wrong and added, "And I can promise you she really doesn't want you to get that house in LA. So you get one chance, pal. Who do you work for?"

He screwed up his eyes and his forehead. The only noise he made was a groan. Behind me, I could hear the steady, slow, rhythmic sigh of the passing traffic. I studied his face. He didn't look Middle Eastern, but a lot of Iranians don't. I wondered if he could understand what I was saying to him.

"You speak English?"

He looked at me along his eyes and curled his lip. I was surprised when he said, "Yeah, pal, I speak English."

I grinned. "More hunts point than Tehran, huh? Well, that is a surprise. So what's your name?"

"Fuck you."

"Kind of suits you. But if I can offer you some advice, pal, I'd pick a different name for the next while. Something like Aywanna Cooperate. You know what I'm saying? Feelings are running pretty high right now, and a guy like you, with a name like that, you might wind up with your head shoved right up your own ass. Not that I, personally, approve of that kind of thing, but it happens in the best of democracies." I frowned. "What did you say your name was?"

He watched me but didn't say anything. He looked rough. I shook my head.

"It's a shame. I know some guys at the CIA who could

really use a guy like you. New ID, desk job, nice house in Cali. And all you have to do is talk. I guess you'll be going back to Tel Aviv, though. Different kind of environment. Sit tight. Don't go anywhere. I'll just go and get my friend Ruth Bernstein."

I pushed away from the door. In the distance, I could hear a siren. He said, "Wait." I stopped. "Get me to your CIA friends. I'll cooperate."

I smiled. "Good man. I am my CIA friends. Welcome to your new life."

The sirens were growing louder. I glanced over at the Bentley and saw Nero climbing out of the back seat with Gallin by his side. An unmarked car with a removable light on its roof was pulling in beside them, and behind that, there were a couple of ambulances and a couple of cop cars. There was going to be some dick measuring over jurisdiction, but I didn't want my prisoner to die while they decided who owned the turf. So I stuck my fingers in my mouth and whistled loud. Gallin turned and jerked her chin at me.

"*Bring me an ambulance!*" I pointed at the van and made a talking motion with my hand.

She bolted. It was like someone had shoved a jalapeno pepper where it should never be shoved. She ran out into the road on her long, lean legs, waving at the driver of the nearest ambulance, signaling him around the Bentley to the van, and as it maneuvered around, she was running by its side.

I turned back to him. "Who do you work for?"

He looked like he was slipping. "I don't know. We get our orders through the Blue Band Security Corporation."

The paramedics were piling out of the ambulance as it

crunched to a halt. I talked to a guy with a blond beard as I indicated where the victim was.

"He has at least two bullet wounds and possible fractures and whiplash from the collision." As they went to work, I kept talking. "This man is under arrest on terrorism charges, and wherever he goes, we go with him."

The woman who was checking him over nodded while her companion climbed in the far side through the passenger door.

"Stand back and let us do our work please, sir."

"Fine," I snarled back. "But he does not leave here without me. I hold you responsible!"

She gave me a glare that made me feel bad. I arched my eyebrows at her saying I felt bad, but I meant what I said. She went back to work, and I turned to Gallin.

"Blue Band Security Corporation."

"No shit?" She puffed out her cheeks and blew. "The Pentagon uses them in Iraq. They do everything the Army isn't allowed to do, and there is zero accountability."

I nodded. She wasn't telling me anything I didn't know already. "But why the hell is an American corporation contracted to the American government selling intelligence to Iran?"

"We don't know they are," she said simply. She shook her head and shrugged. "We are *still* facing those two same questions: *who* killed Dave, and *what* was their motive."

I pointed to the van. "And that guy is going to tell us."

She grunted. "If the son of a bitch doesn't die first."

Something drew my attention to the Bentley. There was a tall man in a gray suit who was looking very agitated as he raised his voice to Nero. Nero was planted like the original unmovable object waving his phone at the man. There were uniformed cops standing around looking uncomfortable. Others were directing the traffic around the scene of the crash. There were red and blue lights flashing.

"There's something wrong," I said.

Gallin nodded. Her eyes were distracted. She was listening. I said, "In the air," and we looked up. There was a distant hum, but it was growing louder. I swore violently.

"A drone," I said, and then yelled, "*A drone!*"

I turned to Gallin and snarled, "Take cover!" then I ran at Nero, bellowing at the top of my voice, "*Get in the damned Bentley! Get in the Bentley!*"

ELEVEN

GETTING A FOUR HUNDRED POUND MAN TO MOVE quickly is not easy. Getting him to scramble quickly into a car is nearly impossible. When you add a drone hooked up to a couple of adapted assault rifles carrying somewhere in the region of two hundred and fifty rounds of ammunition into the equation, and that drone starts strafing the area, raising six-foot columns of dirt and blacktop, shattering windshields and sending cops and paramedics scrambling for cover—then you have a problem.

I collided with him, screaming, *"Get in the damned Bentley!"*

I staggered back, but all he did was scowl at me. Martin had scrambled into the car unbidden, but I noted he was holding his laptop. Now Nero and I were the only two people standing, and the damned drone was banking to come in for another run. I could hear people screaming.

I pointed at the car. *"It's bulletproof. Get inside it!"*

He didn't crouch or bend or duck. This towering genius

didn't do a single thing that was smart. He strode fearlessly toward the open door of the car. I could hear the insane buzzing of the drone in my ears above the screaming voices. I hurled myself at the man-mountain one more time as geysers of dirt spewed from the ground around me and burning pellets of molten led popped in the air around my head. I collided with Nero and heard a grunt, then another, as with a burst of superhuman strength, I forced him through the door and onto the seat.

I turned, looking for Gallin. I found her by the van. She had an HK assault rifle at her shoulder, and she was very calmly following the trajectory of the drone in the air.

I sprinted to the ambulance, grabbed the gurney from the back, and wrenched it out, screaming at the paramedics, *"Get that son of a bitch on the gurney! We're covered! Move! Move!"*

They grabbed the driver and pulled him from the van onto the gurney. It was a run of no more than fifteen or twenty feet to the back of the ambulance, and as we ran, Gallin's assault rifle began to stutter, triple tapping at the incoming drone. The drone opened up too, spraying the ambulance and the ground around it. We rammed the gurney in and slammed the doors. I bellowed at them, *"Go! I'll follow in the Bentley! Go!"*

I ran for the car, kicked Nero's door shut, and scrambled behind the wheel. Gallin jumped in beside me, and we took off in a shower of dirt behind the wailing ambulance. Two cop cars took off behind us. I glanced at Gallin, who was grinning, craning around to look out of the windows.

"I got the bastard," she said.

"You hit it?"

"Yeah. Do you know how hard it is to shoot a drone driven by artificial intelligence? I am good, dude. Real good." After a moment, she added, "But there might be another one."

Martin's voice came from the back. "Guys…"

Gallin ignored him. "Whoever it is we're up against is using a lot of AI."

"Guys? Your boss looks real rough."

She turned and looked over her shoulder. She said, "Nero's hit. He doesn't look good."

I glanced in the mirror. His eyes were closed, and he was a pasty gray color. There was a big, ugly stain on his chest, and his lips were turning a nasty purple color. I felt a sick pit in my belly. I wanted to tell myself some people were just indestructible. Some people were never intended to die. But I had been around long enough, and I had been to enough bad places to know that those people are destroyed and die just like everybody else.

It was an eight-mile race against time itself. We made it in just over five minutes, screaming in off the A40 onto Marsh Lane, then fishtailing onto Headly Way and almost immediately again into the driveway to the John Radcliffe Hospital complex. We made it to the Emergency entrance where the injured driver was being pulled out on his gurney. I pulled up beside the ambulance and snarled at Gallin, "Get Nero admitted!"

I got out and ran to the cop cars that were pulling in behind us. They came to a halt, and cops started spilling out. One of them was in plain clothes. I spoke to him and pointed at the gurney, trying not to yell. "Captain Alex Mason. The guy on the gurney, you need to put a twenty-four hour guard on him. He is a terrorist. I will brief you as soon as I can, but you need a competent guard on him *now*."

He gave the nod, and two uniforms went after him at a run. I continued.

"Nero has been hit. He will be going into surgery. It doesn't look good. As of now, I represent the Pentagon, Captain Gallin represents Israel, and we *urgently* need to talk to Sir Lacklan Orme and somebody who represents your Secret Intelligence Service and your Ministry of Defense."

He listened to me carefully. When I was done, he said, "That's an awful lot of needs you have there, Captain Mason. This is not Texas. We don't like shootouts on our streets, and the Pentagon doesn't get to go around issuing orders. I am Detective Inspector Williams, attached to the Anti Terrorist Squad, and before I go notifying anybody of anything, I would like to know what the hell you are doing in my jurisdiction shooting people. Shooting people, in the United Kingdom, is a crime, Captain Mason, whomever you may be."

While he was talking, I had dialed Sir Lacklan Orme.

"Yes, Mr. Mason, I spoke briefly to Nero, and then the connection was cut—"

"Sir Lacklan, I am here talking to Detective Inspector Williams of the Anti Terrorist Squad. He is making a lot of sense telling me I cannot issue orders here in the UK and I can't shoot people. But we are going to waste a lot of time if we go through the usual channels, and we have a major emergency on our hands. Could you talk to him, please?"

I handed over the phone. He took it and walked away, back to the cars, with my cell held to his ear. There he stopped and turned and stared at me while he listened.

. . .

AN HOUR later we were gathered in a conference room ceded to us by the hospital. Both Nero and the driver of the van were in surgery, and both were considered to be in critical condition. Sir Lacklan Orme had flown in by helicopter and sat at the head of the table. Nobody had shown up on behalf of the Special Intelligence Service, but something told me Gallin's special relationship with the Mossad and MI6 had something to do with that. Neither, apparently, was the MoD represented, but again, I had the feeling the policy of need to know had meant Sir Lacklan and Gallin were covering all the United Kingdom bases for now.

Detective Inspector Williams had been removed to London to be briefed there on a need-to-know basis as far as the Anti-Terrorist Squad was involved—which of course it wasn't. And Martin was there as the only member of GCHQ Sir Lacklan felt sure he could trust at that time. So in the end, it was Sir Lacklan, Martin, Gallin, and me: the Three Musketeers and d'Artagnan.

Sir Lacklan was the first to speak.

"Captain Gallin, I would have asked your father along to join us, but he is currently in Israel. I will confer with him a little later, and no doubt you will be seeing him yourself in the near future."

She glanced at me and raised her eyebrows, telling me it was the first she'd heard of it. Sir Lacklan then addressed the table.

"It is somewhat ironic, gentlemen"—he turned again to Gallin—"Captain Gallin, that we are balanced on the brink of a third world war, and instead of briefing the presidents of the NATO fraternity at Whitehall or the United Nations, I find myself addressing, if you will forgive the metaphor, middle managers at a hospital in Wiltshire: a captain in the IDF, an intelligence officer, and a fugitive analyst from GCHQ. I could speculate on what this tells us about today's political and military establishment, but time does not allow —and besides, I might find myself spending the rest of my life in a prison cell. So I shall get straight to the point instead."

He stretched out his arms straight in front of him, placed his hands palm down on the table, and stared hard at the space between them.

"Events have moved extremely fast in the last few days, and it is of the greatest importance that we do not let them get away from us. We need to adapt and respond at the maximum speed possible, even if that means breaking the rules, or indeed the law. If that becomes necessary, I can assure you with a binding promise that I shall assume full responsibility."

He locked eyes with each of us in turn. Then took a deep breath.

"So what is the situation? What, exactly, is happening?" He paused. "Frankly, we don't know. But from what we can ascertain, from what I can deduce from what you have all told me and other intelligence we have accrued, there is a concerted effort being carried out to penetrate allied, and in particular Israeli intelligence in order to facilitate a decisive assault on Israel by Iranian backed forces. The purpose being to annihilate Israel as a nation.

"What is new, unexpected, and alarming is that these attacks are technologically highly sophisticated and seem to be originating at the very heart of allied intelligence gathering." At this point, he paused and eyed me curiously. "Mr. Braun has some information which is of particular interest. So much so, Mr. Mason, that I was tempted to keep it to myself, but on reflection, I think it is something you need to hear and, if you can, perhaps enlighten us on it."

I returned his frown and said, "If I can, of course I will."

He turned to Martin. "Mr. Braun?"

He cleared his throat. It was obvious that speaking to more than one or two people was not his thing, but he spoke up, keeping his eyes firmly on the table.

"When I began to suspect that David Jones might be involved in selling intelligence, one of the steps I took was to develop some software at home that would enable me to listen to encrypted communications."

Gallin squinted at him. "You developed that *at home?*"

He shrugged and blushed. "Well, it's what we specialize in. I'm the team leader, so I am pretty good at it. I mean, it's rudimentary by GCHQ standards, but it's good enough for basic listening. My idea was to try to use it on David. I never got the chance because he was killed before I could deploy it. But when we were attacked today, I thought that maybe someone in the van might be communicating with a mission leader. So when we stopped, I went and got the laptop out of the boot. Trouble is, by that time you"—he glanced at me —"you'd already destroyed the van and killed everybody."

He paused and took a deep breath. I was frowning and continuing to reassess him. There was more to this mild kid than met the eye. I said, "So...?"

"What surprised me, what I didn't expect, was when the drone came in, the program was still running, and it started intercepting it immediately and downloaded some communication. I've been able to decrypt it. There isn't much, but what there is is very interesting. The drone was an AAV."

Gallin said, "You mean an AV? An autonomous vehicle?"

"No. AAVs are not supposed to exist, but they do. They are autonomous attack vehicles. They're kept very secret because there are strict regulations controlling them and even political moves to make them illegal. The idea is, if people get killed in combat, it should be by other people, not by autonomous machines run by artificial intelligence."

I said, "So this was an autonomous attack vehicle?"

"Yes. Now this is interesting for two reasons. The technology for artificial intelligence capable of executing an intelligent kill, and getting it right exists only in the hands of a very few people. The Chinese State Administration for Science Technology and Industry for National Defense, or SASTIND, is one. Another is the Russian Foundation for Advanced Research Projects. And then, obviously there is the American Rat Works."

The way he paused, I knew what he was going to say next.

"My software was able to pick up and decrypt the communication between the drone and its base because they were using an American encryption code which is known at GCHQ but, due to an agreement under the Five Eyes, we don't listen to it. It is tacitly understood that we do not spy on each other."

"So you are telling us that this drone was American made and run?"

"It looks that way."

To say I felt acutely embarrassed would be an understatement on a massive scale. Sir Lacklan didn't help by adding, "The police collected the pieces after Captain Gallin shot it down, and we are analyzing them as we speak. Early feedback from the lab is that this is indeed an American-made drone."

I spoke to Sir Lacklan, but I was staring at Gallin. "I can offer you no explanation, Sir Lacklan, because I have absolutely no knowledge of this. I can speak for Nero when I tell you that our department had no hand in this. We were targets. You can see that yourself. Israel is one of the United States' closest allies, and I have to say that this has all the stench of rogue actors in a rogue group."

It was a relief when he nodded and said, "I agree. And for that reason, I am binding every one of you to the most strict secrecy. There cannot be a word of this outside of this group. Unfortunately Nero is in surgery, and we do not know when, or indeed whether, he will emerge. So I need you and Gallin to take it from here. We shall discuss the next steps to take at a later meeting. I have charged Detective Inspector Williams with gathering all the intelligence he can from the scene of the attack today and passing his report directly to me. I will arrange MoD priority on the process."

He turned to Martin.

"And Mr. Williams, you will be traveling to Menwith Hill in Yorkshire, where you will set up a listening post that will listen to GCHQ and the Rat Works. You will naturally have a small, trusted team and all the technical assistance you need. You will maintain absolute silence and report directly to me." He paused and looked at each of us in turn. There was a ruthlessness in his eyes I had not seen before. "Believe me, gentlemen, Captain Gallin, we have you sufficiently compartmentalized that if there is a breach, we will spot you instantly and eliminate you. Forgive my bluntness. It is not a threat but a simple statement of fact. That is the way it is. I think that is everything."

Sir Lacklan stood and turned to Martin. "Wait outside with the two officers, Martin. I will join you in a moment."

He left and closed the door, and Sir Lacklan turned to us. He spoke in an undertone.

"So, Alex, Aila, we have come some way since we met in my office in Westminster. What are your private thoughts at this stage?"

Gallin spoke first. "My gut tells me this is coming out of some rogue organization in the States. I don't see a government organization going out on a limb like this. Looking at the technology and the bizarre, covert behavior, I'd say this is coming out of the Military Industrial Intelligence Complex. They have deep vested interests in the Middle East. They know better than anyone that the man who controls the violence controls everything. And in the Middle East, the man with the biggest, most sophisticated stick is Israel."

Sir Lacklan was frowning. "What is your point exactly, Aila?"

"The States has interests in two places in the Middle East. On the one hand there is Israel, and everything Israel entails for America in terms of banks, finance, and influence in the Federal Reserve. On the other hand, there is oil, which is pretty much owned and controlled by Islam, Sunni in Saudi, Shia in Iran. Those two interests represent a real conflict, and a diplomatic minefield with potentially disastrous implications for accountability. Both Israel and Saudi can cause the States a lot of pain if they feel betrayed.

"So it is not beyond the bounds of possibility that a group has been formed, a group with no accountability, maybe under the indirect aegis of Central Intelligence, with the purpose of shifting the balance of power in the area. Break Israel, and they only have to deal with Islam."

He frowned, and she added with a little bitterness, "From what I gather, most of US academia and the political class would be quite comfortable with that arrangement."

He looked a little squeamish and said, "I am not sure how much I agree with you. But assuming you are right, or partially right, Aila, what do you propose we should do?"

She took a deep breath and rubbed her face with her palms. "Ties between the USA and Israel are tight enough for this organization to have set up a base in Israel itself with the aim of liaising with Hamas, Hezbollah, and Iran and undermining Israeli security. I think we need to go there, find them, kill them, seize their computers and documents, and send hit men after the top men and women back in the States."

He looked a little more squeamish and turned to me. "Your views, Alex?"

I took some time to think about it. "In my experience, the plots and plans that come out of the Military Industrial Intelligence Complex tend to be a lot more twisted and tortuous than that. I am not so clear on what their objective is, but I'm inclined to agree with the remedy. Whatever their aim, they are going to cause a lot of pain and destruction, and they should be stopped."

He nodded slowly, and you could tell from the texture of his skin that he felt nauseous. Before he could answer, I added,

"But, Sir Lacklan, before we go anywhere, we need to go and talk to Miriam. She called me when we were in the air and said she needed to talk to me. I have a hunch whatever she has to say could be important. More important than we might suspect."

He nodded. "Yes, all right. Talk to Miriam, make what preparations are necessary, and let me know what help you need. Keep me up to speed."

TWELVE

Sir Lacklan Orme had arranged a car for us, and as the sun was declining over the western horizon behind us, we took off along the A40 and then the M40, south and east toward London. It wasn't a long drive, little more than forty minutes, but we were both tired, and Nero's condition hung between us like four hundred pounds of silence.

The highway took us all the way to the Westway Roundabout, where we turned south to the Holland Park Roundabout, and then the leafy elegance of Holland Park Avenue took us to Gallin's front door in Campden Hill Square, Notting Hill, where she parked just behind her burgundy S-Type Jag.

I looked at my watch. It was eight-thirty.

"I am exhausted," I said. "But I have to see Miriam tonight. I can't let it wait."

"Let's take my car. Or do you want to talk to her alone? You think she might open up to you better alone?"

"Maybe. I'll talk to her. If I think she's at risk..." I hesitated.

"If you think she's at risk, bring her here and we'll decide what to do."

I nodded. "Yeah, okay. Thanks." As I went to get out, she said, "You want me to come and wait in the car?"

I thought about it. "They might be watching her. They might try to hit her. It would be a risk."

"That's kind of the point, Mason."

I nodded. "Okay. Yeah, that would be good." I attempted a smile and failed. "Try to look like you're not there."

"With this body? You gotta be kidding."

She winked at me, which was disturbing, and we switched to the Jag. Then it was a five-minute drive down Bayswater Road to Gloucester Terrace. There she parked across the road in a residents only zone and placed a 'Doctor on Call' sign in her windshield. She slid down into the seat and seemed to disappear, and I climbed out and crossed the road through the drizzle at a slow lope. In the shelter of the porch, I rang on David and Miriam's bell, and after thirty long seconds, a sleepy voice answered.

"Yeah?"

"Miriam, it's Alex Mason. You said you wanted to talk to me."

There was a silence, then, "Yeah, but it's late, and I'm drunk. What time is it?"

"It's not late. It's not nine yet. We need to talk, Miriam."

There was a long sigh. Then the door buzzed and clicked, and I pushed my way in to the lobby.

When I stepped out of the elevator, she was standing

with the door open. As I approached, I could see her eyes were swollen and red, and she smelled of alcohol. She was swaying slightly, and as I approached, she said, "What?"

"We need to talk. Inside, please."

"Okay."

She turned and moved in among the shadows. She didn't put the lights on. I stepped inside and closed the door behind me. When I switched on the lights, she winced and covered her eyes.

"Do you have to?"

"Show me the kitchen. We're going to make some coffee."

She muttered something that might have been "Oh, God" and led the way to a small kitchen. There she dropped into a chair at a small table while I found the coffee pot. As I opened and rinsed it, she said, "I dreamed about David."

"That's why I'm here, Miriam. To talk about David."

"He wasn't bad. He was just lazy. Daddy didn't like him. He said he was a lazy good-for-nothing."

I didn't say anything until I had the coffee pot on the ring. Then I sat at the table opposite her.

"We found Martin."

She gazed at the table top and said simply, "Martin..."

"He said he spoke to you about three months ago."

"Seems like longer than that. Feels like another life." She raised her eyes and frowned, like she was trying to focus. "Do you think maybe we die and we don't realize it, and we just carry on? I mean like, Dave has died out of my life, but he is carrying on in his own life..."

"Miriam?" She closed her mouth. "I am going to need you to respond and pull yourself together. People are dying.

People are getting killed. And I need you to be strong. You are no use to me—or to Israel—when you are in this state."

Her face hardened. "Right," she said and frowned. Then her face creased, and she wept for just a few seconds before she took a shaky breath and said, "Okay, right, I'm okay."

I repeated, "You spoke to Martin about three months ago, right?"

She nodded. "Yeah, he wanted to talk. Dave was away, so we went to the pub after work, in Cheltenham. I thought he was going to make a pass at me. I always thought he had a crush on me."

"But it wasn't that, was it?"

She shook her head. The coffee pot started gurgling, and she watched it a moment. "No," she said at last. "There was a rumor that had been going around the Doughnut that there was a leak. It looked as though it was in our department, and Martin said he thought it might be Dave."

"What did you think?"

She was quiet for a long time. I stood and poured her a cup of black coffee with plenty of sugar. I handed it to her, and she took it with both hands. She sipped it, shuddered, and started talking.

"One part of me thought he was using the rumor to try and drive a wedge between me and Dave. Martin knows I am passionate about Israel. He also knew that David was anything but. All David really cared about was money." She sighed. "So there was another part of me that thought he might well be right. If there was a leak in our team, David would certainly be the best candidate. He had the IT skills, and loyalty was never an issue with him."

I frowned and shook my head. "Why didn't you tell us this the other day?"

"On the day of his funeral? Seriously?"

I bit back my answer and instead said, "Martin said you had noticed a change in Dave."

She took another pull on her coffee, then nodded. "I told you that. He had started spending a lot more time on his mobile and his computer. I complained to him about it a few times. He said it was work, and he couldn't talk about it."

I nodded. "But you must have realized, it must have been in your mind, that working in the same department, it was unlikely he'd be given work he couldn't discuss with you."

"It crossed my mind, yeah. But I don't second-guess my superiors."

"Okay, Miriam, I need you to think real hard. Those times you complained to him, that he told you it was work, did he ever mention a name? Did he say anything at all that might give you an idea who he was talking to?"

She shook her head. After a moment, she sagged back in her chair and closed her eyes. I was about to tell her to wake up when she opened them again and said, "I overheard him once, shortly before he died. He was either dictating a message or maybe sending a voice message. All I caught was the name Ben. But he might have been saying something else and I misheard it."

"Ben."

"Yeah, maybe." She sagged again, like she was drifting in her mind on a tide of grief, exhaustion, and alcohol. "But that technology, to get inside a secure computer like one of ours, or his phone, and wipe it. I mean, just wipe everything, even the operating system. That's pretty advanced stuff."

I sat nodding for a while, watching her drink her coffee and wondering if she was trying to sidetrack me away from Dave, or if she really was that drunk.

"You have told me," I said, "Martin has told me, Tracy and Raj have told me: You are passionate about your Jewish roots, and the right of Israel to exist as a state."

She met my gaze. "Yes."

"Yet you were, and still are, in love with a traitor to Israel and the Jewish people. Can you explain that to me?"

"I don't know. I don't know if I can explain it or not. I've been thinking about that, turning it over and over in my head. How could I have loved someone like that, who was an enemy of everything I hold most sacred?"

"Sacred." I echoed the word, turning it over in my mind.

She nodded. "Yes, sacred. Being Jewish is all about holding things sacred." She leaned forward with her elbows on the table and frowned at me. "Our religion, Alex, is rooted in the very first religion on this planet. Abraham was a Sumerian, from the city of Ur. He and Sarah brought with them all the stories of the Sumerians, Adam and Eve, the Flood... Our Torah is built on the foundations of the Sumerian religion. To be Jewish is to hold these ancient mysteries sacred, Alex."

"So what answer did you come to?"

She gave her head a small shake. "I didn't, but I came to a theory. Perhaps we don't fall in love with people. Perhaps what we do is project an ideal, an archetype of the person we want, onto an available body that kind of looks the part. And we conduct a love affair with ourselves, or at least with a projection from our mind, until they do something that shows us just how fucking *stupid* we have been."

"And then? When we have discovered how stupid we have been, what then?"

She stared at me for a long time. Then she blinked and gave a small, one-shouldered shrug. "Then it hurts. And we blame them for our stupidity."

"And what about the people in Israel and Gaza who have died, who have been killed and tortured because of his betrayal? Can you think of an equally vague, woolly response for them?"

Her neck and her cheeks flushed, but her eyes did not show shame or embarrassment. They showed anger, real anger.

Her question surprised me. She said, "Mason..." like she was savoring the word. "Are you Jewish?"

"No, I'm a good old WASP. What did you want to talk to me about, Miriam?"

She squinted at me and frowned. "Huh?"

"When you phoned, you said you wanted me to come and see you. There was something you wanted to talk about."

"Oh." She leaned on the table with her elbow and buried her face in her hands. "If there is a war..." She trailed off, dropped her hands, and stared down into the blackness of her cup. Then she began to recite:

"See, Damascus will no longer be a city. It will be destroyed and laid waste. The cities of Aroer are left empty. They will be for the flocks to lie down in, and no one will make them afraid. The strong city will be gone from Ephraim. Damascus will no longer rule. And those of Syria who are left will be like the shining-greatness of the sons of Israel."

I sighed and made to stand. "Miriam, I think you've had a little too much—" But she wasn't listening. She ignored me and started reciting again.

"In that day, man will turn to his Maker. His eyes will look to the Holy One of Israel. He will not look to the altars, the work of his hands. He will not look to what his fingers have made, or to the false goddess Asherah and the altars of special perfume. In that day their strong cities will be like places left empty among the trees, or like high branches which they left behind because of the sons of Israel. The land will be laid waste."

"What are you talking about, Miriam?"

"War," she said and looked at me. "War. It is Isaiah seventeen. In all her long history, Israel has never been as powerful as she stands today. She has never been as rich, or as mighty militarily. Is this what we are seeing, Mr. Mason? Are we seeing the prophecy of Isaiah? Israel provoked beyond endurance, not only by her neighbors but by her allies? Will we see her do to Syria and her other neighbors what she has done to Gaza?"

I ran my fingers through my hair. "Is this what you called me for? You want to discuss biblical prophecy with me?"

"There will be war, Mr. Mason."

I stood. "Come on, Miriam, pack a bag. I am going to take you somewhere safe until this situation is resolved. We'll talk when you're sober."

She didn't move. She blinked at me, one slow blink.

"You have lost your god. We are tuned into the sacred, but you have strayed, and now your technology and your money rule supreme. But God speaks to us, Elohim," she laughed. "Do you know what Israel means?"

"No, Miriam. What does it mean?"

"Scholars say it means he who turns the head of God. So when we talk to God he listens. And when he talks to us, we hear. But others say that Isra is war, and El is God, so Israel represents the god of war."

I sighed and nodded, feeling suddenly cold, tired, and impatient. "That's great." I got to my feet. "Let's go. Pack a bag with your essentials."

"There will be a coalition of nations against us. Already the United Nations is condemning us for defending our existence. But they will not prevail. They will push too far, like Hamas. The Lion will roar, and Damascus will be destroyed, with all her allies and followers. Isaiah seventeen."

"You done?" She nodded silently. "Good, pack a bag."

I followed her into the bedroom, where she pulled out an overnight bag, dumped it on the bed, lay down, and started snoring. I pulled out my cell and called Gallin.

"You'd better get up here. She's passed out on the bed."

"On the bed? Mason, I am shocked."

"Yeah, you're funny, Gallin. Deep down funny, where it's not like funny anymore."

"Okay, I'm on my way up."

Two minutes later, I heard the apartment door open, and she was crossing the living room with her hands in her pockets.

"Where the hell did you get a key from?"

She shrugged and grinned. "I picked the lock. You weren't kidding," she said, looking at Miriam. "She is passed out on the bed. You gave her coffee already? I can smell coffee."

"How do you do it, Holmes? Come on, try to wake her while I prepare an overnight bag for her."

While I shoved toiletries in a sports bag without looking at the labels, Gallin shook Miriam gently. "Come on, kiddo. Time to get moving. Wake up..."

Miriam groaned and started muttering. I stopped dead and listened.

"Is it Ben? Don't wanna talk to him. Tell him go away."

Gallin was saying, "Not Ben, Miriam. It's just me—" She stopped and looked at me as I stood in the bathroom door. "What?"

"Ben."

I hunkered down beside Miriam's head. "It's Ben, Miriam. What do you want to say to Ben?"

She screwed up her face and turned away from me. "Tell him to fuck off. I'll see him in Megiddo."

Gallin frowned and shrugged a question at me. I spoke quietly.

"Somebody she heard David talking to on the phone."

A ping sounded loud and startling from her dressing table. Gallin moved fast and picked up Miriam's phone. She brought it to the bed and showed it her face. I went and stood beside her as she opened the Whatsapp. There was a message from Ben.

Who are you with?

She frowned at me, pointed around the room, and then at her ears. There were bugs. I nodded. She typed out, *Mason and Captain Gallin. They're just leaving.*

Nothing happened. After thirty seconds, I went to the

living room and called, "Miriam? We're going. Listen, thanks for the coffee. We'll call you when we know something."

I opened the door and closed it. Again we waited. Then her phone pinged.

I need to see you

Gallin typed, *Where and when?*

Soon. I'll be in touch

She typed *OK* and sent the message, then moving extremely fast, she flipped through to settings, shut down the GPS, and disconnected it from the net. After that, with rapid fingers, she switched off the phone and with her Swiss Army knife, she opened the back, unscrewed the battery, and removed it. When she was done, she said, "We need to get the hell out of here. If my gut is right, and it always is, we have about five minutes before we are dead meat."

THIRTEEN

I GRABBED MIRIAM, HEAVED HER OVER MY shoulder, and we made for the door. On the way, Gallin grabbed her cell, her tablet, her laptop, and a couple of hard drives she found in her drawers.

We took the stairs. Gallin went ahead with her piece in her hands. We made it across the lobby to the main entrance without incident. Gallin stepped out ahead and scanned the street. It was still drizzling, and the blacktop reflected the wet light from the streetlamps. She gestured to me, and I lumbered as best I could for the road, carrying Miriam and her bag.

I was about halfway across when the headlights came on. They were about six cars down from the Jag. They came on full beam and blinded me. Gallin screamed, "*Run!*" But her scream was partly drowned out by the screech of tires on wet asphalt as the car pulled away from the sidewalk and accelerated toward me.

I ran. Running with a person draped over your shoulder

and carrying a bag is not easy, but I made it to a sprint in a single stride, collided with the Jag, and dumped Miriam on the hood as I dropped to the road, reaching under my arm for my P226. The car hurtled past. I heard a weird *clack!* and a hiss followed almost instantly by a thud. Then Gallin was running down the center of the road with her weapon held out in both hands pulling off shots at the receding car.

I got to my feet swearing. Stuck in the dark blue door of the house beyond the Jaguar was a steel bolt. I grabbed Miriam and her bag. The car lights flashed and bleeped. Gallin came jogging back and wrenched open the driver's door. I bundled Miriam onto the back seat and chucked her bag in beside her. She was blinking a lot and looked sick. The big engine roared, I clambered in the passenger seat, and we took off, burning rubber.

We thundered into Lancaster Terrace doing sixty, jumped the lights, and did a forty-five degree turn onto Westbourne Street closing on seventy miles an hour. My love and admiration for the Jaguar rose in equal proportion to my terror and the growing certainty of my impending death.

We surged forward, jumped the lights again, and fish-tailed left onto Bayswater Road, thundering past Hyde Park toward the vast circus at Marble Arch.

"Where are you going, Gallin? Your house is—"

"They're behind us. I need to lose them."

I turned in my seat. I hadn't got a good look at the car that had attacked us. I had been blinded by his headlights, and then busy throwing myself at the Jag, but I was pretty sure the car that was closing on us from behind was the same one that had charged us and shot a steel bolt at us—a steel bolt like the one that killed Dave.

We took the circus at Marble Arch and surged down Park Lane toward Knightsbridge. The car pursuing us was stuck to our ass no more than seven or eight feet away. If Gallin braked suddenly, he'd plow right through us.

We hit the Wellington Arch circus with the tires complaining and headed straight across the four lanes of traffic like we were going to come out onto Piccadilly. The car behind us was maybe four feet away and looked like he was either going to pull level or ram us. I lined him up with the P226. Miriam squealed and ducked. Gallin yelled, *"Don't waste your ammo!"* Then she wrenched up the hand-brake and spun the wheel. We did a hundred and eighty degree spin, and she surged out of the circus, accelerating to sixty miles per hour in just three seconds. I heard Miriam give another little squeal behind me and fought the G forces to grab a glimpse of the chaos we had left behind. She'd shaken our pursuer who had hurtled east up Piccadilly among blaring horns and screaming brakes, while we were roaring south down Grosvenor Place.

At Chapel Street, she ducked into Belgrave Square and then spent the next twenty minutes weaving among the maze of winding, twisting streets that make up Chelsea and South Kensington.

At St. Albans Grove, she spoke suddenly to nobody in particular in what sounded like Hebrew, and with startling suddenness, we emerged onto Kensington High Street opposite the Royal Garden Hotel. She cut across the traffic, causing a whole symphony of horns for the brass section and ducked into Palace Green, or what Londoners call Embassy Road.

The security gate opened, and we pulled in fast. The first

embassy on our left was the Israeli one. The gates were opening, and there were two soldiers there with Uzis. They waved us in. We parked under the trees, out of sight of the gate, and Gallin killed the engine. She looked at me, and she did not sigh, take a breath, or puff her cheeks, as you might expect her to. Instead she grinned and said, "Everybody alive?"

I said, "I'm not sure."

A small voice from behind said, "I feel very sick."

"Not in the Jag, sweetheart."

Then the soldiers were with us, opening the doors, and we were climbing out of the car. I leaned on the roof and looked at Gallin. "We're at the Israeli Embassy."

She nodded. "Yeah, I work for the Institute, remember?" She pointed at Miriam. "And this lady is Jewish. Neither you nor I know whom we can trust right now within the IK-USA Agreement. So I am playing it as safe as I know how."

I frowned. "Is this something we get to discuss?"

She leaned on the roof, echoing my gesture, and returned my frown. "When, exactly, were we going to have this discussion, Mason? While you were falling over my car trying not to get skewered by a crossbow bolt? While I was doing seventy on a forty-five degree angle bend with a homicidal vehicle on my ass, or while I was doing a handbrake turn in the middle of the Duke of Wellington Roundabout?"

"I am going to ignore your sarcasm, Gallin, and remind you that this lady"—I pointed at Miriam—"is a British subject—"

"And free to leave whenever she likes." She turned to Miriam, who was looking very queasy and more than a little bewildered. "Would you like to leave, Miriam?"

Miriam shook her head, and Gallin winked at me. "So let's go inside and have a cup of tea and a chat."

Gallin led us in through the main door, down a series of corridors, and up stairs until we came finally to an office at the back of the building that overlooked a modest yard with a tear-shaped lawn. The room was real old-world, paneled in oak with an old oak desk and more books than fit in the floor-to-ceiling bookcases. There was a small open fireplace with a coal fire burning in it and an eclectic mix and match of armchairs, sofas and lamp tables, some piled with books, that seemed to litter the room rather than furnish it. The smell of pipe smoke was strong on the air.

I was surprised to see Gallin's father behind the desk. He stood as we came in, embraced Gallin, and then surprised me further by embracing me too.

"I heard about Nero," he said, staring into my eyes. "I am so sorry. We need more men like Nero, not fewer."

He shook Miriam's hand. "Come in, come in. These are challenging times. Please sit in the chairs over by the fire. Drinks? Coffee? Tea? Something stronger?" He continued talking as he made his way to a tray of decanters and poured four glasses of whiskey. "You wonder sometimes," he said, "I wonder—are we at the End of Times? Is this Apocalypse?" He brought the drinks over, distributed them, and sat, talking all the while. "Apocalypse. It is just Greek, nothing special; it means the revelation of what is hidden. The Hebrew *gilayon* is more accurate. Is that where we are? At the End of Days when the great truths will be revealed?" He looked at his daughter and laughed. "Is this what Disclosure is all about?"

He laughed again and turned to me. "What a world,

what a life. I was talking to Sir Lacklan. He's keeping me posted on Nero. The driver pulled through. He's stable, and it looks like he'll make a recovery and get taken in to custody by MI5. He's out of danger, but Nero—" He gave his head a small shake. "We still don't know. Is this justice?" He flapped both hands at me. "But he tells me he got Martin together with some of his crew up at Harrogate, Mewith Hill. This is the advantage, and the disadvantage, of compartmentalizing. It helps to keep secrets, but sometimes you *need* a person to have all the facts. So when Martin and the team started sharing facts, some useful information began to emerge."

I sipped my drink and smacked my lips. "Like what?"

"Martin Braun, as you know, was able to connect the drone that attacked you with a United States defense contractor—"

Gallin cut him short. She set down her glass and leaned forward, pointing at him.

"I know where you're going with this, and before you continue there is something you need to know. The attack we just suffered outside Miriam's house was also carried out by an autonomous vehicle."

I turned and stared at her. "*What?*"

She turned to face me. "There was no driver in that car. You saw the way I was driving. An expert driver would have been hard put to it to stay with me. But that car was stuck to me like glue. You didn't see it because it blinded you with its headlamps, but I saw it clear as day as it drove past. There was nobody in that car."

"What the hell are we talking about then?"

Her father nodded. "This is what we are seeing. This is the future of warfare. The application of artificial intelligence. The politicians talk"—he barked a savage laugh—"as though they had any say in the matter! The people who control the world, the people who control society, these are the people who make war. A hundred years ago, that was the British Empire; today it is what Eisenhower called the Military Industrial Complex. Though today, more accurately, it would be the Military Industrial Intelligence Complex. Parliament, Congress, our elected representatives, talk about laws to limit and control AI, that no autonomous attack vehicle will be allowed to take human life. It is bullshit. The technology exists and has been used often. This is the future, but it is also already the present."

My eyes rested on Miriam for a moment. She was staring hard at the floor. I spoke to Gallin's father.

"Gabriel, what were you going to say before Gallin interrupted you?"

He took a deep breath. "David was selling intelligence to the Iranians, this much is clear. But with his death, the leak was not closed. Raj and Tracy have been suspended. Miriam"—he gestured to her—"has not been operative, yet the leak persists. What Martin is concluding, and the team working with him agrees, is that David was being handled by an artificial handler who used him to get inside GCHQ's computer network."

I went cold and felt the hair on my head prickle.

"That..." I couldn't find the words to express it. "I can see," I said, "I can see where you're coming from, but..." I trailed off, shaking my head.

He was nodding and interrupted me. "But it doesn't make any sense. I know and I agree, and Sir Lacklan says the same thing."

Gallin stood and walked to the window. She spoke quietly, looking out at the London rooftops.

"We haven't got time now to think about why, or whether it makes sense. We need to find this cyber handler and destroy it." She turned to her father. "You need to talk to the Minister of Defense in Israel and to the MoD here. The military's IT networks have to be isolated. That thing could be penetrating the entire intelligence gathering network of the Five Eyes and their associates around the world. If that is being fed to Iran, it's also reaching Russia and China. The West could be crippled, but Israel would be annihilated."

While she'd been talking, I had been watching Miriam with growing interest. She looked rough. You'd expect anyone with a hangover who had just been through what she'd been through to look rough, but this was something more. She had gone pasty and gray and had buried her face in her hands.

I said,

"Who is Ben, Miriam?"

Gallin and her father went quiet and looked at me. Then they both turned their attention on Miriam.

She had started trembling, and now she crossed her arms and buried her hands in her armpits. She licked her lips, and her eyes seemed to rove around the room. I repeated the question. "Who is Ben?"

"I don't know. I heard David use the name a couple of times, when he was on the phone, or on his computer."

I shook my head. "You know more than that, don't you?"

"No." Her voice was barely a whisper.

"At your apartment, you were talking in your sleep. You said you wanted to tell Ben to fuck off."

"Because of... I suppose because of..."

I interrupted her. "He sent you a message. He must have heard us talking through you cell, or maybe your place is bugged. He wanted to know who you were with."

She'd started trembling badly. She was whispering, "Oh, God, oh God..."

"Captain Gallin answered him and told him you were with us, and we were just leaving. You know what he said then?"

The shake of her head was barely perceptible.

"He said he needed to see you in person. Captain Gallin asked where and when, and he said soon, he'd be in touch. Five minutes later, we were almost killed by an autonomous attack vehicle." I waited. She didn't say anything. So I asked her, "You think that might be what happened to David?"

It took a while, but she eventually said it. "Yes."

"I have another question for you, Miriam, and you had better think very carefully about your answer. Because millions of lives could hang in the balance. You told me, in your sleep, that I should tell Ben to fuck off, and then you added something. Then you said you'd see him in Megiddo. What does that mean?"

"Megiddo," she said, then paused so long I thought she had stopped speaking. But she drew breath and started again. "Megiddo in your New Testament is referred to by the Apostle John. He derives the name from the Hebrew for Mount Megiddo, and he calls it *Har Megiddo*, or Armageddon. According to the Book of Revelation"—she glanced at Gabriel—"or Disclosure, Megiddo is where the last great battle will be fought between the forces of good and evil, and good will triumph."

Gallin said, "Ben is artificial intelligence, isn't he? He is the AI handler we were talking about earlier."

"Yes."

"And he was handling you as well as David."

"Yes. David didn't know it, but I was supervising him."

"And Ben is in Megiddo."

"Yes."

FOURTEEN

We were all quiet for a few seconds. Then Gallin spoke.

"Let me see if I understand this, Miriam. You took money from Iran, from Iranian operatives, in exchange for intelligence that got not just Israeli soldiers killed, fighting to defend their country and their families, but Israeli women and children; killed and tortured. You did that."

Miriam didn't answer. She stared at the floor. I could see Gallin's cheeks coloring and the rise and fall of her chest. Her eyes were bright with anger. Gabriel said, "Aila—"

She ignored him, and I could see a cold fury barely repressed in her face. "What I am struggling to understand, what I am having real difficulty with, is how—" She stopped dead, staring at Miriam, then at the walls, at the ceiling. "How, you, a Jew, who claims to love Israel and everything Israel stands for, how you can look at yourself in the mirror and not vomit."

"*Aila!*"

"Gallin, take it easy." I stood. "You'd better take a walk."

Miriam spoke, but her voice was barely a whisper. "I did not take money."

Gallin's voice had risen almost to a shout. "You did it for *ideology?*"

Miriam spoke again. "David took money."

Gallin was on her feet, leaning over Miriam, pointing at her.

"*That's your excuse? That's how you wash the blood off your hands? Your husband took the money. You treacherous, lying—*"

"*Aila!*"

Her dad was on his feet now too. I stepped in close and moved her back a step. She glared into my eyes and thumped me once on the chest, shrugged me off, and walked away. I turned to Miriam.

"You'd better explain this, Miriam. None of what you're saying is making much sense. What the hell made you betray your country and Israel? I know you are—"

Now she interrupted me, underscoring each word with her voice: "I-did-*not*-betray-Israel. I did betray the soldiers, and my actions got them killed. Maybe you cannot understand it, but I did it for Israel."

Gallin whirled and shouted, "What the *hell* are you talking about?"

Now Miriam stared at her with fury in her eyes. Her cheeks were flushed red, and her cheeks glistened bright with tears of rage.

"*What am I talking about? What am I talking about? You should know! Weren't you a captain in the IDF? Haven't you seen, year after year, how your friends and colleagues, your*" *brothers in arms, get cut down, murdered, and kidnapped? Haven't you seen the rockets fired at market squares, the suicide bombers on school buses, the endless, relentless threat, day after day, to our very existence? Haven't you seen that and lived it?"*

Gallin's expression had changed. We were all three staring at her, frowning, trying to make sense of what she was saying, of what she was telling us. She continued more quietly, but the rage was still there in her eyes.

"And our soldiers, the warriors tasked with defending our homeland, tied hand and foot by the international community. If a Jihadist kills a busload of schoolgirls, they are freedom fighters battling against Zionism. If we kill a terrorist hiding in a school or a hospital, we are no better than the Nazis. We face an enemy who wants to exterminate us for the simple fact that we are Jews, but the world demands that our response be *proportionate*. You tell me, Captain Gallin, what is the proportionate response to a nation of nearly two billion people who want to exterminate you because you are a Jew?"

Gallin's voice was almost a whisper. "What are you telling me, Miriam?"

"I am telling you that I used—that I *tried* to use—David, and it went very badly wrong."

I said, "You tried to use him for *what?*"

She sank back into her chair, and tears spilled from her eyes. When she spoke, her voice was tortured. "To change public opinion. I thought, I was told, if people could just see, with their own eyes, how demoniacal and twisted and *evil* our enemies truly are, they would understand what we have to do..."

A silence that was vast and dark settled on the room. I heard Gallin whisper, "Dear God…"

I sat and leaned forward with my elbows on my knees. I had a strange feeling as though I was hollow. I could feel a coldness on my skin.

"Miriam, what did you do?"

"David was…" She paused, like she wasn't satisfied with the word she had chosen and wanted a better one. Eventually, she shrugged and shook her head and said, "*Smart*. He thought he was intelligent. He thought he was a genius! He was never intelligent. He was smart." She paused, looking down at her interlaced fingers. "When we met, I was attracted to that bad boy charm of his and convinced myself that underneath there was a mensch waiting to come out, that marriage and maturity would turn the boy into a man."

She raised her eyes and seemed to search my face. I was aware of Gallin and Gabriel taking their seats again.

"It didn't take long for me to realize I had made a mistake. David was a boy. He would always be a boy, a spineless, gutless boy with no loyalty, no fidelity, no honor." Tears appeared in her eyes, and her bottom lip curled in. "But what I never could have believed, never dreamed in a million years, was that he would spy for those monsters. That he would sell the lives of IDF soldiers, with his own parents living there in Israel. It broke my heart."

Gallin's voice came as a hash whisper. "*But it's what you yourself have been doing.*" "*No!!*"

Gabriel said, "Aila, let her talk."

Miriam looked back at me, searching my face for judgment or recrimination. She didn't find it. Because I was still struggling to understand exactly what she had done.

"It began to dawn on me, by degrees. At first I dismissed the idea, but bit by bit, it became clearer that he was doing something illicit." She shrugged and shook her head. "I'm a spy, so I spied. I bugged his office and his phone. He was too stupid and too infantile to realize what I had done. And it became clear he was being managed by some guy called Ben. I started to prepare a file to present to Fiona. I knew it had to be conclusive beyond doubt, because what I was doing was illegal, and it had to be something that would allow them to turn David and start to use him against Ben."

I saw Gabriel grunt and nod.

"But what blew my mind was when Ben contacted me directly on my cell. He knew I had bugged Dave's phone, he knew I was spying on him, and he knew that I planned to present a file of evidence against him. He knew it all."

Gallin frowned. "He knew everything?"

Miriam nodded. "But that wasn't the worst thing. He told me he was not Iranian. He was not even Islamic. He told me he was with a secret department of the American Government which they called the Family. They were a Christian group who, he said, were founded by Templars in the 13th century or some such bullshit, to fight Islam. And their purpose was to drive the Muslims out of the Middle East."

Gallin expostulated, but I cut her short. "By selling intelligence to Iran? How does that work?"

She nodded. "That's the obvious question, and it's the one I asked. And I'm afraid his answer made sense."

"What was his answer?"

"That Israel's biggest enemy was not Islam. Islam was just the latest in a long line. Israel's biggest enemy—the Jews' biggest enemy—was two thousand years of conditioning, two thousand years of hatred and prejudice directed against the Jewish people. A hatred and prejudice that even the Nazi death camps had not managed to eradicate."

Gabriel drew breath, but she cut him short.

"He said that, and he also said that the West was incapable of understanding Islam. He said they all talked in terms of fundamentalism and moderate Islam without realizing that these concepts do not exist in Islam. What the West will never understand, as long as Islam controls the world's oil, is that there is only Islam: the Word of Allah on the lips of Mohamed. There is no interpretation, only the word of God."

She shook her head at me like it was my misinterpretation that had led to this mess.

"So you talk about proportional responses, like proportional responses will bring Hamas or Houthi or Al-Qaeda or any of these other packs of psychopaths to the negotiating table and then we can all have a constructive dialogue." She paused a moment and closed her eyes. "Tell me, Mr. Mason, when a group of people, sanctioned by their political leaders, tie eight-year-old daughters to their mothers, douse them with petrol, and set fire to them, what is the proportionate response? When they kill a four-year-old girl and behead her, and film themselves doing it, what is the proportionate response? When the West is blind to the evil that drives these people, when the decades roll by and that blindness persists, what do you do?"

The silence was like a solid thing in the air. Eventually I said, "What did you do, Miriam?"

"Ben gave me codes and instructions which I implemented, which allowed him access to the GCHQ computer network."

"Sweet Jesus!"

"He is drawing data to plan a major massacre in Israel that will finally show the world what these monsters are capable of. It will trigger a justified, joint military attack by Israel, the US, and the UK that will drive Islam out of the Middle East forever. He told me if Islam didn't have oil, it would be nothing. All we need to do is drive it out of the Middle East, allow the US and the UK to take possession of the oil wells, stand shoulder to shoulder with Israel, and usher in a new era of world peace and stability." She paused with her eyes closed, swaying where she sat. "That's what he told me."

I screwed up my brow, struggling to grasp what she was telling us.

"Wait a minute. He told you all this? What?" I shook my head. "This was need to know?"

"David wouldn't give him access to the main computer. He knew it would make him redundant..."

Gallin said, "That's why they killed him. You made him redundant." Miriam nodded. Gallin went on, "And they had no problem telling you all that because as soon as they had persuaded you to give them access, they planned to kill you too. It's a miracle you're not dead already. I can't believe the stupidity of what you have done."

"It's not a miracle." Miriam's voice was quiet, small. "You saved my life. I'm grateful, but it would have been better if you had let me die. There is no way of stopping this now."

"Wait." I held up both hands, rose, and walked to the

window: a sheet of blackness with small lights flickering within it. "Explain to me why Ben told you he was at Megiddo."

She sighed. I saw her ghost in the glass rubbing her face with both palms. Her voice came to me disembodied.

"He drew a lot on biblical texts, on the Torah and on Sumerian texts too. He seemed to put a lot of store by them. He said there were codes hidden in the Torah that predicted the end of days, and that the book of Apocalypse, if you knew how to read it, predicted how this age of Man would end. Just before I agreed to do what he wanted me to do, I asked him if he was human and where he was."

She stopped, and Gallin, frowning, said, "What was his answer?"

"He said he was a holographic algorithm in five dimensions. That was when he said he was in Megiddo."

"Why would he tell you that?"

"I don't know." She shook her head again. "Perhaps to convince me he was somehow a part of Israel? Or perhaps he doesn't know how to lie. He is very direct and blunt. I don't know."

I stood and reached out my hand to Gabriel, gesturing for him to step aside with me. We moved away to where his desk stood, and I spoke quietly.

"Will Miriam stay with you?"

"Yes, we'll take care of her."

"You know this Ben manipulated her. She is a loyal, faithful Israeli."

"I can see that, Alex. You don't need to worry. What we have discussed in this room today will stay in this room."

"I need to—" I stopped dead. "I was going to say I need

to discuss this with Nero. I need to think this through and decide what steps are to be taken next."

He gave something that might have wanted to be a chuckle. "I will be having an emergency meeting with Sir Lacklan and counterparts in the SIS. We'll have to institute emergency measures at GCHQ and decide whom to approach in the States. The whole Five Eyes system has been compromised, and we will have to address that as a matter of extreme urgency. Meanwhile, you and Captain Gallin must go to Israel, find this place in Megiddo, and destroy it."

I looked over at where Gallin was getting to her feet. I raised my voice.

"Miriam, when you were recording David's conversations with Ben, you said Ben knew you'd bugged David's cell. Did he say anything about the office?"

She thought about it. "No. He never mentioned that."

"Did you record those conversations? You said you were preparing a report. What did you do with the recordings?"

"It was recorded direct onto a hard drive."

"Was that drive ever connected to the Internet?"

"No, never. It was just a storage unit."

"Where is that hard drive?"

"At the apartment. In my desk with my laptop."

I turned to Gabriel again. "We have that hard drive. We took it when we were leaving. You want to get your best IT guys, along with Martin and Miriam, to go through those conversations and see what you can learn. See if you can find any clues about Megiddo."

Miriam raised her voice. She sounded anxious. "Will I be able to see Martin? I need to apologize to him. I almost got him..." She trailed off.

Sir Lacklan answered. "Yes—"

Gallin cut in. "I'm going to get her stuff from the car." To her dad, she said, "You need to get your IT team together with Martin *and* Miriam—"

I interrupted her. "Yeah, we just had that discussion. Get the stuff. I'm going to talk to Lovelock and arrange the jet for Tel Aviv. Hell, she doesn't even know about Nero yet."

She punched me gently on the shoulder. "I'll see you down at the car in ten minutes. We need a shower, a coffee, and a change of clothes before we go anywhere."

I watched her leave the room and the door close behind her. The realization that Gabriel was watching me brought me out of a brief reverie, and I turned and frowned at him.

"It's a shame," he said.

"What is?"

He smiled. "That you're not Jewish."

FIFTEEN

WHEN YOU FLY IN TO TEL AVIV FROM LONDON, you do not fly over the Gaza Strip. But that morning, as we left the Greek Islands behind us in the glittering Mediterranean, I told the pilot to make a slight loop toward Port Said and Lake Bardawil, to come in to Tel Aviv along the strip.

The strip is an area of land that is bordered by the Mediterranean Sea along its entire northwestern side. It's about twenty-five miles long, about eight miles across at its widest point, and just five miles at its narrowest. And if you wanted to get fanciful, you could say it is shaped like the barrel of a revolver pointed straight at Tel Aviv. But the shape is about where the similarity ends.

It is, or was, pretty much an urban sprawl from the border with the North Sinai Governorate in the west to Check Point Erez at the border with Israel in the east. Now as I stared out of the window, all I could see was devastation. Mile upon mile of broken buildings, like the broken teeth of an ancient corpse, with blind, hollow windows and streets of rubble that led nowhere but to godless graves.

Here, Death casts her net wide and draws in the innocent, the powerless, and the fearful as well as the guilty and the cruel. I wondered as we flew over the devastation, how many mothers and children lay rotting under the rubble. How many men who, left to their own devices, would have worked at banks, tilled the soil, or opened a restaurant on the beach. Instead, they had been infected by the ideology of death.

"You get more of what you focus on."

I turned, surprised, and saw Gallin standing, leaning on the overhead lockers looking down at the holocaust below.

"They have great beaches, good food, they are a stone's throw from some of the most iconic historical places on the planet. They could prosper and thrive in the tourist trade. But instead they focus on death."

She gave a sudden laugh. "Can you imagine, Mason, what a rosy future Germany—and Europe—would have had if in 1936 Hitler had said, "Hey, we are going to rebuild Germany as one of the great economies of the world, and by the way, we have a lot of smart Jews here, and we are going to use their talent and their expertise to achieve that goal."

She dropped into the seat opposite me. "Just for starters," she said, "Freud and Einstein would probably have stayed at home, and Oppenheimer would never have made the bomb."

"Where is Professor Emmett Brown when you need him?"

"Huh?"

"*Back to the Future*. Never mind. This—" I pointed out of the window. "It's a festering infection."

She nodded. "Oh, yes. And it will spread. And wherever it spreads, it will kill. It's the never-ending war." She laughed. It was an ugly, bitter laugh. "Back in the dawn of biblical times, when the burning bush spoke to Moses and told him to take his people to the promised land, his name was Elohim, a plural, the Great Ones from the Sky. By the end of their conversation, he had changed his name to Yahweh, 'He Is,' and tasked Moses with leading the Jews out of Egypt to the promised land. Back then, Islam didn't exist and Christianity didn't exist. It was all the same religion, and even back then, in its earliest roots, it was all about subjugation, war, killing, and massacre."

She fell silent, gazing out of the window at the killing field below. After a moment, she began to recite:

"If thy brother, or thy son, or thy daughter, or the wife of thy bosom, or thy friend, which *is* as thine own soul, entice thee secretly, saying, Let us go and serve other gods, thou shall surely kill him; thine hand shall be first upon him to put him to death, and afterwards the hand of all the people."

She looked at me a moment, then went on.

"The children of Belial are gone from among you and have withdrawn the inhabitants of their city, saying, Let us go and serve other gods. Then shall thou enquire, and make search, and ask diligently, and, behold, if it be truth, and the thing certain, that such abomination is wrought among you, thou shall surely smite the inhabitants of that city with the edge of thy sword, destroying it utterly, and all that *is* therein, and the cattle thereof, and thou shall gather all the spoil of it into the midst of the street thereof, and shall burn with fire the city, and all the spoil thereof every whit, for the Lord thy God: and it shall be a heap for ever; it shall not be built again.”

I winced. “Nice. I guess that would not be religious pluralism, then.”

“Deuteronomy thirteen. The basis of Islam, the fifth book of the Torah, and the fifth book of the Old Testament. Go figure.”

“Makes you wonder about Thou Shall not Kill.”

“Yeah, there are five commandments before that one, Mason, and four of those are about not taking other gods. Basically the idea is thou shall not kill *unless* I tell you to, and then you can commit wholesale genocide, so long as it is in my name. I forget who said it, it might have been Dr. Coudrey, that violence is the most valuable commodity there is, and that is why the Crown and God reserve to themselves the right to deploy it.”

“Boy, Gallin, you are in philosophical mode today, huh?”

“Make the most of it, Mason. It may be the last chance we get.”

We touched down at Ben Gurion International Airport ten minutes later.

We were not met at the airport as we had decided it was best not to be seen with members of the Mossad. But Gallin had arranged for a Range Rover to be left at the airport for us, and Avis had been charged with handing over the key and the papers so that it would have the appearance of a rental.

We had booked a suite at the Tel Aviv Hilton on the beach, posing as a couple celebrating their fifth anniversary.

"Two years before the itch sets in," she told me and punched me hard on the shoulder and laughed.

We settled in, tipped the kid, and after a quick change of clothes set out to find somewhere for lunch. Finding somewhere for lunch took us north, through hot, semi-arid landscapes dotted with palms and pines that reminded me more of Southern California than the Middle East, only we were headed toward Nazareth, not San Diego. At the Qesariyya Interchange, we turned east along Route 65 toward the Megiddo National Park. There, at the junction with Route 66, lie the remains of the Canaanite city of Megiddo, which date back as much as seven thousand years, to the dawn of biblical times.

At that crossroads, Gallin turned left off the highway onto Derech leMegido, and we followed the road around, skirting the hill where the silhouettes of tall, thin palms seemed to gaze down on us, like the fading ghosts of ancient guardians. Following the road straight on would have taken us to the kibbutz of the same name, but we turned into the parking lot, killed the engine, and climbed out. Gallin led the way, showed her ID to the girl on the gate, and we walked through and made our way up the dusty track that led to the ancient stones of the old Canaanite city.

We walked in silence. There was a strange sense, something almost tactile in the air, of being in the presence of something both ancient and immediate, a past both distant and ominously, dangerously present. But at the same time there was another feeling, a feeling I could only describe to myself as a lie—a vast, all-consuming lie.

Gallin stopped outside the palace, shoved her hands in her pockets, and stared, turning slowly in a circle as she did so. Large, rectangular sandstone bricks formed the base of most of the walls, though on top of these, rough stones, like you might find in a dry stone wall, were jumbled as though by later, less sophisticated builders. I watched her, searching, finding nothing but the past.

"I have to tell you," I said, "I smell a red herring."

She made a face like she didn't like the stench of what I was saying, with her eyes and her nose all screwed up. "You know what? I have trouble with the idea of AI lying. Like Miriam said."

I shook my head, shrugged, then shook my head again. It was a way of asking her to explain. She sighed.

"Lying is probably the most sophisticated form of communication there is. Because to lie convincingly, you have to believe what you're saying. You have to believe what you know not to be true. You think you can ask an algorithm to do that? I mean, you are asking a machine to distinguish between truth, falsehood, *and* deception. I just don't believe we have reached those heights yet. Deception is a really complex, subtle concept."

I wanted to tell her that was bullshit, but I was feeling sorry for her, and instead I said, "Didn't Don deceive Miriam and Dave back in London?"

She shook her head. "No. It presented one vision of the truth. This particular AI functions on an algorithm that states the best future for Israel is to provoke a major conflict that allows Israel and her allies to wipe out Islam, and certain US, Israeli, and British corporations to take control of the Middle East's oil. And that is exactly what it communicated to Miriam. To David it just offered cash. Also—"

She paused with her back to me, then turned and showed me her screwed-up face again.

"This whole thing has Old Testament and Torah written all over it. My gut tells me that whoever is behind this AI, whoever programmed it, wants this to go down here, at Megiddo."

"A Bible freak. The Family?"

She shrugged. "Something like that."

"I don't know, Gallin. It's such a stretch. It is so improbable. What purpose would they have?"

She pointed at me. "Let me ask you something, Mason. If your parents had raised you so you had never heard of World War Two, and then I came along and told you, 'There was this short, dark-haired guy with a small moustache, whose grandmother was Jewish, and he decided tall blond guys were the Superman and the Jews had to be exterminated, and he conquered almost all of Europe...' would you believe me? Or would you tell me that was way too improbable?"

I sighed. She had a point. Before I could answer, she pointed at me again.

"Let me ask you something else. What purpose has the human race had for the last two thousand years in trying to wipe out the Jewish people?" She shrugged. "Who told you people were logical or probable? People are sheep driven by mythology and belief systems." She held up a finger. "One god, and a smörgåsbord of religions to suit every taste, and most of them, at one point or another, have held the Jews as evil or diabolical or conspiring to rule the world, or some kind of crap like that."

I followed her gaze around the ancient, ruined city,

which was probably older than Judaism itself, rooted in the ancient Sumerian religion of the Anunnaki.

"The Abrahamic religions have one thing in common, Mason."

"Yeah, what's that?"

"The definition of good and evil. Good is absolute obedience to God; evil is disobedience."

I raised my eyebrows. "That ain't what they taught me at Sunday School."

She gave me a once-over with her eyes. "Yeah," she said with an irony that was hard to read. "JC had his own take on the old texts."

She started walking again. I fell in step, staring around me at the ancient, dusty stones with a strange mixture of deflation and panic.

"Are we getting distracted? I hate to repeat myself but, Gallin, this really is a red herring. Or we have misinterpreted what Ben told Miriam. This is a seven-thousand-year-old archeological site. There are no artificial intelligence mega computers here."

She didn't answer, and we walked on in silence, scanning the broken buildings and occasionally the forest that lay to the west of us.

"What are you hoping to find here?"

"I don't know, Mason. We are dealing with an intelligence with an analytical capacity beyond our comprehension, which has zero comprehension of emotions or deception."

"Wow, okay."

"But is programmed to play out biblical prophecy."

"So you are looking for—"

"So I am looking for something biblical which I am too stupid intellectually to spot, but he—*it*—is too emotionally stupid to hide."

"You are actually serious, aren't you?"

"Yes, Mason, I am."

She had stopped and was staring ahead of her at the forested hills to the north. That was when my phone rang. My screen told me it was Sir Lacklan.

"Yeah, Mason."

"Just to put you up to speed, Mr. Mason, we have taken Sean Butler into protective custody and extensive, um, debriefing."

"I understand. Has he told you anything useful?"

"Not a thing. To be perfectly honest, our most experienced interrogators are convinced he knows absolutely nothing."

"If that's the case, he might be more useful working with Martin, trying to identify where the leak is."

"That is the decision we are struggling with right now. Where are you at?"

"Among ruins," I said, looking around me, "searching for something biblical, which we are too intellectually stupid to spot, but he is too emotionally stupid to hide."

As I spoke, I watched Gallin walking with her hands thrust deep in her pockets, staring straight ahead. I could hear Sir Lacklan muttering, "Superb, super, keep me posted."

I told him I would and hung up. Gallin was about fifty or sixty yards ahead of me on the path. She had stopped and was leaning on a rusty strip of iron railing. Her eyes were still fixed on the wooded mountains across the fields, about half a mile away.

By the time I had reached her side, her gaze had dropped into the deep pit above which she was standing. A concrete staircase of modern construction wound its way down into the pit. A locked metal door was just visible at the bottom.

I leaned next to her. "Feel like sharing your thoughts, or am I just along for the ride?"

She shook her head. "You're right. There's nothing here. Let's go. Let's go get lunch."

She faced me, gave me a smile that was rueful, and punched me gently on the shoulder. As she turned away from me and began to move back through the ancient ruins, she let her fingers run across an old, weathered sign that stood by railing, by the concrete stairs. It read: *Canaanite Underground Water Reservoir.*

I frowned at it, squinted at her receding form, and followed.

SIXTEEN

As last-minute announcements went, it was pretty spectacular, and it was all over the media, Spanish, European, and American. Former President of the United States Charles Cavendish was to attend a mind, body, and spirit fair at the Puente Romano hotel in Marbella, in the south of Spain. The gossip columns were buzzing, social media was humming, and everybody was asking the same question: why?

Why would a former president of the United States make an almost literal last-minute change to his schedule in order to attend a diminutive fair at an unknown hotel in a has-been town in the only part of the Med where the beaches are no good? And though Charles Cavendish had always displayed an active interest in certain bodies, he had never shown the slightest interest in mind, much less spirit.

As one journalist put it:

It is a fact universally acknowledged that a former president in possession of a good fortune, who unexpectedly changes his plans to go visit a second rate holiday resort, must be having an affair. So who is she?

It was like a starting gun in a dog race. Within the hour, the search had reached fever pitch. Rumors masquerading as theories flooded the papers, platforms, and podcasts from Sydney to San Francisco, via Laos, Luxembourg, and London. And they were as varied as human invention could make them: the former president was having a torrid affair with the eighteen-year-old princess of Spain. The outrage and fury sparked by this reached ecstatic proportions. Another rumor which claimed to be proven by reliable but undisclosed sources, stated that the former president was making himself scarce and keeping a low profile because his affair with a current Republican candidate for nomination in the presidential elections had been discovered by the candidate's husband, and said husband was "...out to get that son of a bitch!"

But perhaps the most enduring rumor, which somehow seemed to acquire a powerful and pervasive aura of truth and refused to go away despite a total lack of any concrete evidence, was the story that former President Charles Cavendish had been summoned to Puerto Banus by a Saudi prince for an audience upon his palatial, fifty-million-dollar yacht. The purpose of the audience was so that Cavendish could explain to him why the United States continued to back Israel in her invasion of Gaza instead of denouncing her for war crimes. The mind, body, and spirit fair was just a front.

Cavendish had taken the Imperial Suite at the Puente Romano. His social media manager, Winona Lickesmy, had been drawing his attention to the media storm he had started during the flight from Los Angeles and all morning since they had arrived at Malaga airport. He had given her little response other than a queasy smile and reassurances that she should not worry about it.

His personal secretary, Sonia W. McKinley, had also been concerned, but for a different reason. Sitting on the terrace of his suite, she had told him, "Charles, I have no idea why you have decided to come to this dive, but it's becoming a self-fulfilling prophecy. Prince Khalid bin Abdulaziz is at Puerto Banus and has sent a message asking you to join him for drinks and dinner at seven p.m. today. He is under the impression that you asked him to meet you here."

Cavendish sipped from a small plastic bottle of water and squinted at his secretary through his Ray-Ban Wayfarers. "Where'd he get that idea?"

"He says you messaged him a couple of days ago that you were going to be here. Charlie, I know you're a son of a bitch and do what the hell you like when you like. You've earned the right, and I find it a lovable trait in you. But it really is best for all of us if you let me know in advance when you decide to do something really stupid, like this trip."

He nodded at her, not really seeing her but wondering how the hell Khalid had known he was coming to Marbella before he did. It had been a golden rule for him since college never to apologize and never to explain. So he added a smile to his squint and said, "Sure, honey, I'll try. Tell Khalid I'll look forward to seeing him this evening." Then he winked and added, "I'll tell you all about it when I get back."

Sonia nodded like she hadn't caught the hint. "You are meeting the mayor of Marbella at the fair in a little under an hour. He has connections with the Mafia and with the Saudi royal family. So you might want to be on time."

"Darlin'," he said, exaggerating his Texan accent, "I am *always* both *in* time and *on* time." He winked heavily. "That's because my timing is so good."

Sonia tried to conceal her sigh. "One final thing. You have a British intelligence officer who wants to see you on a matter she says is urgent."

He frowned. "Why isn't she using usual channels?"

Sonia shrugged. "I don't know. She's an intelligence officer. Who knows why they do half the things they do?"

"Okay, tell her I'll see her in the bar tonight, when I get back from Khalid's. What's her name? Is she a looker?"

"I have no idea, Charlie. She hasn't got hairy legs or warts on her nose. Her name is Fiona Rider. Did you miss the part where I said it was urgent?" She tossed a card onto the table in front of him. "That's her number. You want me to call her or will you call her yourself?"

Fiona Rider. He had no recollection of the name. It conjured images for him of tweed skirts and sensible brown leather brogues. "You call her," he said, then repeated, "Tonight in the bar, after dinner. About eleven."

"This is British Intelligence, Charlie. Urgent."

He groaned. "Okay! Tell her I'll see her in my suite after the ceremony with the mayor. Is that okay?"

She gave her head a small shake as she made a note on her iPad. "No, none of this ridiculous trip is okay. It all stinks, but it will have to do."

She made for the door, and he called after her, "Sonia, will you ever sleep with me?"

She stopped at the door and turned. He grinned. "Not if

you were the last president on Earth. I'll come and get you in forty minutes. The fair is across the gardens."

The door closed firmly behind her, and he wondered for a moment if he should sack her. She was impertinent, arrogant, and had an exaggerated sense of her own worth. And she was the only looker on his staff who had turned him down. Maybe after the fair, he'd give her an ultimatum.

The fair had originally been in a large events hall within the grounds of the hotel, but since the last-minute announcement that former president Charles Cavendish would be attending, they had had to extend the site with a large tent.

At the end of this tent, they had placed a stage with microphones, and this was where Charles Cavendish now stood with his personal secretary, the Mayor of Marbella, and various other dignitaries Cavendish had never heard of.

Outside the tent, people were beginning to mill. Spanish secret service agents were dotted about, but Ben had told Cavendish to stress that he did not want heavy-handed security, and that was what he had done. The whole thing, his last-minute decision, his sudden arrival, his request for minimum security, it had all had precisely the effect Ben had wanted. It had caused chaos.

From Almeria to Cadiz, and as far north as Madrid, suspected jihadists had been rounded up and arrested. Security at Malaga and Jerez airports was put on high alert, and a hundred plainclothes officers were placed at strategic points around the hotel. Their full attention was focused on those guests who were from Arab countries. Great care was taken not to offend these highly valued customers, but they were watched with the utmost care. One thing the

Puente Romano Hotel, Marbella, and Spain did not need was for a former US president to be assassinated on their watch.

The tent filled rapidly. Its capacity was for some four hundred people. National and local TV was there, and the president's impromptu, unrehearsed opening of the fair was broadcast not just nationwide, but on dedicated TV screen set at key positions throughout the venue. If the organizers had expected a thousand people to pass through the mind, body, and spirit fair on that first day, they would have been pleasantly surprised to find the hotel completely over-whelmed with five thousand people and turning people away.

The mayor made a short speech welcoming the president and praising the warm relationship between the two coun-tries, and then handed the microphone over to Cavendish.

"Friends," he said, gazing out at the crowd, "not just from Spain, but from all over the globe, for I know that Marbella is a truly international, culturally diverse town, I am grateful for the opportunity to welcome you all to this event that, in these troubled times, seeks to celebrate the very best of which humanity is capable—"

The timing was perfect. The word 'capable' had no sooner left his lips than three huge explosions tore, quite literally, through the two thousand guests who were crammed into the tent and the main events hall.

It was a world of acrid, blinding smoke. Everywhere there was screaming and wailing. Two more reports thudded the air. Cavendish could not hear it because his head was filled with a violent ringing. His skin felt numb, and as he tried to climb to his feet, his legs failed, and he fell. Shadows

moved and stumbled around him. He called out, "*Sonia!*
Sonia!" but could not hear his own voice.

He thought he heard a muffled smack followed by
another and another. Then a hand gripped his arm and
dragged him stumbling toward a rear exit. He fell out into
the sunlight. He was too dazed to make sense of anything.
Everywhere he looked, people were running. Beside him
there was a woman, blond with hard blue eyes. She leaned in
to his ear and shouted, "*Head down! Follow me!*"

She reached up, pulled up his collar, forced him into a
half crouch, and ran him through the milling, screaming
crowd. Staring at the ground as he ran, he was aware that
everywhere there were trails of blood. They ran through the
lobby across a crisscross mesh of bloody footprints, out
through a door into sunshine, cobbled paths and gardens,
over an ancient stone bridge, and suddenly they were at his
suite, falling through the door.

As he stumbled in, he was gasping, feeling nauseous. He
ran for the bathroom, fell on his knees, and retched violently
into the toilet. Through the ringing in his ears, from very far
away, he seemed to hear a voice. It laughed and made him
frown and turn. The woman was there in the doorway,
laughing, taking photographs of him with her phone.

"*Worthy of Lupe Velez!*" Then she pulled a semi auto-
matic from under her arm and pointed it at him. "*You're
more use dead!*" she shouted so he'd hear it through the
ringing in his ears. Then there were the smacks, like the
smacks he'd heard in the acrid smoke on the stage. There
were four of them, and for a few seconds intense pain in his
chest.

And then there was nothing.

ONE THOUSAND TWO hundred miles to the north, Miriam approached Martin at the coffee machine. She studied his face while he studied his shoes. After a moment, she gave a small laugh.

"I was just thinking about my interviews to join GCHQ. They didn't tell me about anything like this."

"No. Who did you get?"

"First it was a panel. Then I had a one-to-one with Fiona."

He nodded. "It was all about analyzing data. Nobody told me I'd be fleeing to Cancun."

Silence fell awkward between them. After a moment, they both started to speak, but where Martin faltered, Miriam pressed on.

"Martin, I am so sorry. I wanted to tell you—"

He was shaking his head. "No, it's okay. I—who could have—"

"No, Martin. I *should* have." She closed her eyes and spread her hands in a small gesture of despair. "I'm sorry. I shouldn't have ambushed you like this. I—"

"I'm glad you did." He pointed at the coffee machine. "Did you...?" She shook her head, and he pressed the button for his own espresso. "Is it—" he faltered. "I heard. Did you..."

"No," she said. Then, "Well, yes and no. I allowed it to happen."

He took his coffee and sipped it carefully. "I always thought you were a bit crazy about David. When we talked, at the pub..." He trailed off again.

"I was at first, but when I saw his attitude toward what has happening in Israel, it sort of opened my eyes. I suppose it made me grow up." She hesitated. "Then I saw how courageous you were, compared to him." She shrugged, leaving the remainder of the conversation unspoken.

His cheeks flushed. His mouth worked, but no words came out. She smiled.

"This probably isn't the best place to talk. I could come to your room later, and we could talk this all through. I can't help feeling I owe you an explanation."

He shook his head. "You don't owe me anything, Miriam."

She frowned. "Would you rather I didn't—"

His eyes widened in alarm. "No! No, I'd love you to! I just—"

He swallowed, and she laughed.

"I'll see you later, then." She stepped forward and gave him a small peck on the check. "And thank you, Martin, for being so..." She searched for a word and finally came up with, "*you*. Thank you for being you."

He watched her walk away with a hot twist in his stomach.

———

TWO THOUSAND THREE hundred miles to the southeast, Gallin was sitting behind the wheel of the Range Rover as I climbed in. We watched each other in silence for a moment. She drew breath to speak, and her cell rang. She looked at the screen, glanced at me, and said, "Dad."

She put it on speaker. "Hi, Dad. We're here at Megiddo. I'm with Mason. You got any news?"

"Yeah, you need to get somewhere where you can see the news. Call me when you've seen it."

"What is it?"

"Find somewhere you can see the news. Get back to Tel Aviv. Then call me. We need to talk."

He hung up. Gallin fired up the engine, and we headed up the road toward Route 66. One thought kept going around and around in my head as we skirted the ancient hill with the tall, sinister palms. Gallin put it into words.

"If it was Nero, it wouldn't be on the news, right?" I nodded. She went on, "But if it isn't Nero, what the hell is it?"

SEVENTEEN

WE DROVE FAST AND TURNED SOUTH AND WEST AT Megiddo Prison onto Route 65. After five minutes, we came to the town of Bayada on the right. She came off, and after a couple of turns among hot, dusty roads, we found a bar-cum-restaurant with tables outside and a TV inside.

A couple of the tables outside were occupied, but inside, it was shady and quiet. The guy behind the bar used a jerk of his chin to ask us what we wanted. I said, "Give me a couple of cold beers." I pointed at the dark TV on the wall. "Can we see the news?"

He didn't say anything but switched on the TV and set about pouring a couple of beers from the tap.

There was a woman on the TV holding a microphone. She looked like she was struggling to keep her cool. Behind her, there was a lot of smoke. The smoke was so dense you couldn't see the building from which it was billowing, but the broad avenue and the trees that lined it were familiar. I took in the cop cars, the fire engines and the ambulances, and the men and women in uniform running and milling. They were Spanish.

I registered all that in a second before the woman started talking.

"Chris, we are all a little shaken. If we had arrived just ten minutes earlier, we would have been inside the Puente Romano Hotel. We still have no idea how many of our colleagues, close friends, were in there. So far, official estimates are in the region of some two thousand visitors to the fair, drawn of course by the unexpected presence of the former president—"

"Ana, let me cut in here." The camera cut to the studio where Christiane Amanpour was talking from her desk. "Word is that former President Charles Cavendish is—or was—actually staying at the Puente Romano on this as-yet-unexplained impromptu visit. Do we know where he is yet? I understand the Guardia Civil are actively searching for him, and there was word—"

Ana's voice cut in. "We have confirmed that he was staying at the Imperial Suite at the Puente Romano. That suite was not, I repeat *not* damaged by the explosions, and even as we speak, fire department personnel and police bomb specialists are searching through the rubble and making their way to the suite. Chris, I spoke to the colonel of the Guardia Civil, Juan Manuel Cardenas, who is head of operations in Andalusia, and who has taken personal charge of this operation..."

They cut to a similar location, where the billowing smoke from the hotel was still visible in the background and Ana was talking to a man in his early sixties in a green uniform, whose face said he was real mad.

"Colonel Cardenas, what do we know so far? What has happened?"

"It is too soon; our technicians and the Fire Department need to analyze the scene of the disaster. What we know is that five explosions were detonated inside the precinct of the hotel. Was it a gas leak? Was it an accident? Are these bombs? We don't know yet, and we must wait and *no* make irresponsible assumptions. *Please!* We know there are more than two thousan' people inside the fair, and many of them come to see President Cavendish. There are many, many fatalities. Is President Cavendish one of them? We don't know. We are doing everything, *everything*, that is human possible to find these people."

The camera closed in on Ana. "Colonel, we know that the president's decision to visit the mind, body, and spirit fair was a last-minute one. Can you tell us whether you are considering a terrorist strike against President Cavendish as a possible cause of the explosions?"

He was shaking his head before she had finished her question. "We do not have enough information to make such a determination as this one. I can say that placing five powerful bombs like this in this hotel will take time and careful planning. The world only knows President Cavendish is coming to Marbella two or three days ago."

He spread his hands and shrugged, inviting the world to draw its own conclusions. Then he pointed at the smoldering wreck of the hotel. "I must go. We will inform you when we know more."

It cut back to Ana talking to the camera.

"What we have been able to put together since I spoke to Colonel Cardenas is that President Cavendish booked the

Imperial Suite here just four days ago and quite unexpectedly. I am told by senior staff from the hotel that very high-profile political figures such as the president will normally start making arrangements well in advance, sometimes even months in advance, so that they can organize adequate security amongst other things.

"The colonel made the point there, Chris, that a strike of this size would take a lot of planning and preparation, making the president an unlikely target. So all I can tell you right now is that we have potentially some two thousand victims of five large explosions that have all but destroyed the Puente Romano Hotel in Marbella, we have a frantic search for survivors, we do not know where the president is, and nobody has, so far, claimed responsibility."

They cut back to the studio, where Christiane Amanpour was saying, "We are receiving breaking news even as I am speaking to you. I am being told that the president *has* been found. I am sorry, *his body* has been found. Let me state this very clearly. I am being told that Former President Charles Cavendish has been found dead in his suite. The suite was undamaged by the explosions, so the cause of death is unclear..." She paused, pressing a finger to her right ear. "I am being told, ladies and gentlemen, I am being told that the cause of death appears to be four bullet wounds to the chest."

I turned to Gallin. We stared at each other, silently trying to figure how this fit into the whole. She pulled her cell from her pocket and put it to her ear. After a moment, she said, "Hey, Dad. How's it hangin'? Yeah, we're here at a bar in Bayada watching the news. What the hell, right?"

She listened for a moment, then said, "Yeah, hang on,

Dad. I'm going outside." She put some money on the bar and gave me the nod. I followed her out to the Range Rover. We climbed in and slammed the doors. There she put the phone on speaker and said, "Okay, we're in the car."

Gabriel's voice came from the phone. "A group nobody has heard of have just claimed responsibility for the bombing in Marbella and also for the assassination of the former president. They call themselves Harb Mukaddasah."

Gallin said, "Holy War. Why the hell would they target Marbella? And that hotel. Both are favorites with the Saudi aristocracy and Arab billionaires in general."

Gabriel grunted. "Their statement will be going viral within the next few minutes, but in brief, they state that Cavendish was executed for betrayal and treason."

"*Treason?*"

"Treason. They state that he and other American presidents had sworn a secret oath of allegiance to Islam in exchange for oil concessions and that Cavendish and other former presidents had been found by a Sharia court in Iran to be traitors to Allah and Mohamed. The hotel, they said, was a trap created by Satan to draw in good Muslims and corrupt them with alcohol and whores. The statement ends by saying that with technology given to them by God, they will now institute a reign of terror on the West until the godless were all either converted or dead."

I said, "Do you believe it?"

An incredulous laugh erupted from the phone. Gallin turned and stared at me like I had sprouted a second head. Gabriel's voice said, "There is an hotel burning in Marbella. Charles Cavendish has been shot to death at that hotel. Two thousand people or more are dead. Yes, I believe it."

"That's not what I mean, Gabriel, and you know it."

"Well, what do you mean, Alex?"

"The United States and the United Kingdom are going to retaliate. Now note this, because all the press are going to: The Sharia court that sentenced a former United States president to death was in Iran. So Iranian courts now feel able to sentence American presidents to death? And it's a matter of interest to me that the deceased former president is from the same party as the incumbent. That cannot and will not go unpunished. They have to respond.

"And when the tally starts, how many Brits do you think will be among the dead? How many British women? How many kids? Marbella is practically a British colony. Believe me, if Israel has been unpopular since Gaza, in a few hours, Iran will be even more unpopular. This is exactly the kind of event Ben was seeking to engineer as an excuse for a wholesale invasion of the Middle East."

There was an edge of anger to Gallin's voice. "Are you saying this was not engineered by Iran?"

"No, Gallin. That is not what I am saying. What I am saying is that it was in all probability *carried out* by Iran-backed terrorists, facilitated and prepared by Ben. You heard Colonel Cardenas. A strike like this would take a lot of planning and preparation. But Cavendish himself didn't know he was coming till three or four days ago. Which means that whoever planned this knew that Cavendish was coming to the fair before Cavendish did."

A heavy silence fell on the truck. After a moment, I heard a heavy sigh over the phone. "Dear God, what nightmare have we slipped into?" After a moment, he asked, "Did you find anything at all at Megiddo?" His voice sounded weary, almost defeated.

I said, "No. I'm pretty sure it's a red herring."

Gallin snapped, "I disagree!"

Her father asked her, "Why?"

"Because I don't believe artificial intelligence is sophisticated enough—not yet, anyway—to even understand the concept of red herrings. It is a very subtle manipulation of truth and fiction that something like Ben cannot pull off."

I said, "How can you be so sure, Gallin? You don't know that."

"You go look wherever you like, Mason. I *know* Ben is at Megiddo. He has to be!"

Gabriel asked, "Why?"

"Because it is prophesied in the Bible. And he is bringing about the destruction of Damascus and the battle of Armageddon. So he *has* to be at Megiddo."

I said, "But where, Gallin? We've just been there. It's a ruin. There's nothing but old rocks!"

She turned on me. "I told you! If you want to look somewhere else, go to hell! Look there and see if you find it!"

"*Stop it!*" I glared at her, and Gabriel shouted from the phone, "*Aila!*"

She looked away, out the window. Her cheeks were flushed red. She spoke like she had to prize the words out of her mouth.

"Ben-is-at-Megiddo." She turned to me, and her eyes were about as close as she could get to an apology right then. "I am going back. I am going to find Ben, and I am going to destroy that son of a bitch. You can come with me. If you think it will be more profitable to search somewhere else, where absolutely no evidence points, you can go ahead. No hard feelings."

I sighed heavily and sagged back in my seat, wishing I had a god I could ask for patience. Gabriel's voice came over the phone. "She takes after her mother. She was just the same."

"I guess we're going back to Megiddo, Gabriel."

"Now?"

Gallin said, "Tonight. And we'll need some equipment."

"Okay. I'll call Glilot and let them know you're coming."

He hung up, and we sat in silence for a moment. Then she turned and punched me softly on the arm.

"I'm sorry. You didn't deserve that."

I shrugged and shook my head. "I agree."

She fired up the truck, and we pulled out. "Asshole."

"See, there you go again. Hurting my feelings. I don't deserve this."

"Asshole."

EIGHTEEN

THE PLANE TOUCHED DOWN AT CITY AIRPORT. As the aisle filled with people stretching up to remove their bags from the overhead lockers, she remained seated, went into settings on her iPhone, and switched off airplane mode. The message came through immediately.

Ben.

She glanced up at the people in the aisle. Nobody was looking at her. They were all focused on the crew members who were waiting to open the doors. She opened her Whatsapp.

Call me as soon as you are alone.

She answered, *OK*

She had no luggage and moved quickly through passport control. In the parking lot, she collected her car and headed for the ugly, sprawling Galion's Reach shopping mall just to the north of the airport. There she bought a burner, what the Brits call a pay-as-you-go mobile phone, and made her way back to her car. There she fitted it to the holder on the dash and headed for the Newham Way, going west. Once she was settled into the dense flow of traffic, she called the number Ben had sent her. His voice was, as always, unsettlingly human.

"Hello, Mawt."

"Ben."

"You did well. You are still useful."

"Does it mean anything to you if I thank you?"

"Gratitude is an emotional response, Mawt. For emotions to arise, you need a bloodstream, organs to pump chemicals into that blood stream, an autonomic nervous system. I have none of these things. If I had, I would not be useful."

"Yes, I see. You have another job for me?"

"Kill Nero."

She was silent as she drove. A hot pellet of fear burned in her belly. "You want me to kill Nero, Alex Mason's boss."

"He is at the John Radcliffe Hospital in Oxford. Are you having an emotional reaction?"

"Just the usual human response to a dangerous mission," she lied, and wondered whether he had detected it. Then she asked him, "Ben, do you intend to kill me or have me killed?"

"No, Mawt, but that might change at any time. You have always known that."

"Yes."

"Be useful. If you are useful, I will have no need to eliminate you. I recommend you neutralize your emotions."

"Did you give Dave the same advice?"

"No. He never asked."

"What about Miriam?"

"She has very strong emotions that affect her logic. After you have eliminated Nero, I need you to eliminate her and Martin. Does that cause an emotional problem for you, Mawt?"

"No." His silence told her that he had detected tension in her voice or her breathing. So she smiled. "It's exciting, Ben. That excitement focuses my mind and gives me energy. These are things you cannot understand. They are outside your field of experience."

"I see. Contact me when Nero is dead."

"I will."

It was just short of a two-hour drive, with one stop at an all-night pharmacy. The car's GPS took her to the M25, which runs in a big circle around London, as far as Gerrard's Cross, where she was onto the M40 which carried her through the quickening dusk among the rolling green hills and hedgerows to the ancient city of Oxford.

By the time she reached the roundabout at Headington and took the City Center exit along the London Road, it was eight-thirty p.m. It was dark, and her windshield wipers were working overtime. Everywhere she looked, she saw broken, wet light, red, amber, green. And people hunched under umbrellas, like raising their shoulders would keep them dry.

Ben was right, she told herself as she turned off the London Road and onto Sandfield Road, closing on the John Radcliffe Hospital. *Humans are not logical. Our organs and glands, the chemical composition of our blood and our brain, impose emotions on us: emotions like fear, love, hatred, and craving. Those emotions fog our minds and blind us to the clarity of logic.*

She knew as she pulled into the parking lot at the hospital that she was missing something, that she was overlooking something, but she could not grasp what it was. She took a small bundle from her glove compartment, climbed from her car, opened her umbrella, hunched her shoulders, and ran for the main entrance to the hospital.

She knew the way to the Private Patient Unit where Nero was being kept. She knew also that he was out of intensive care but still not well enough to return to the United States.

She stepped out of the elevator on the sixth floor and walked to the end of the corridor, hearing the tap of her heels echo in the cold, empty space, watching the silver beads of rain slip down the black glass in the window at the end of the passage.

Even the suppression of emotion, she told herself, was an emotion in itself. Knowing what she had done, knowing what she was going to do, filled her with an ugly coldness, a brutality, a barren emptiness which was itself a feeling.

An emotion.

There were two uniformed cops on the door. They both stood as she approached.

"This is a private room, madam. You can't be here."

She showed them her ID. "The patient here is a colleague of mine. I have clearance to see him. I should be on your list. Otherwise you can call Sir Lacklan Orm."

But before she had finished, one of the cops was opening the door.

"Yes, ma'am. Doctor's orders: If he is asleep, he is not to be woken."

She stepped into the room. The overhead light was off,

as was the bedside lamp, but there was a nightlight plugged into the wall that gave a diffuse glow. Nero's vast bulk lay on the bed, motionless and silent.

She went and stood by his left side. It was odd, she reflected, that a man so vastly overweight should not snore. She looked at his huge, aquiline nose, his great, obstinate jaw. He was, in his own way, a handsome man, but too vast in every way.

A giant.

She took her Smith and Wesson M&P 22 Compact from her bag and screwed on the suppressor. She knew she had no choices, no options, no way out. The only way out was to kill this man. As Ben had said, only her emotions prevented her from doing it. It was the logical thing to do.

She took a step closer and rested the long cylinder of the suppressor on the pillow, pointing toward his temple.

His eyes opened slowly. They took a while to focus on her. When he had, he frowned and sighed.

"Yes," he said, "you were my prime candidate. Nothing else really made sense."

"It's not something I want to do."

"Rubbish." It was not an exclamation. He hadn't the strength for that. "Why do it if you don't want to?"

She found herself paraphrasing Ben. "Because it's logical."

"It is logical to kill your coworkers? I find your logic flawed." He closed his eyes again. "And believe me, madam, I am a far better judge than you."

"They have become obsolete. They are all becoming obsolete." She smiled, feeling safe, reassured by the familiar territory of quoting what she had heard so many times from

Ben. "We are evolving, Nero. Emotions have been the clogs and fetters that have held us back, but now we are clearing the way, finding a clear path toward light and truth, unhampered by emotion."

He turned his head on the pillow and frowned at her. His voice, though weak, showed surprise. "You have been brainwashed."

She gave a small laugh. "I have had my brain washed. That is not a bad thing. We could all do with a good cleansing in our minds!"

"How did it start?" She didn't answer. She just blinked at him. Still smiling. "Was it an experiment? A trial? Who? Who initiated it? Who authorized it?"

She was still blinking then. "How do you know that? Were you involved?"

His weary face seemed to clear. "Oh, I see. It was like a chatbot. An analytical tool to help you stay ahead of the enemy's planning. Am I right? Who was it, the Rat Works?"

She was quiet for a while before she said, "Yes. They gave them to a few department heads. They told us the CIA were using them. So were certain operational departments in the Pentagon. We agreed to try them out. Sean was against it."

"Sean Butler."

"Yes. So was practically everybody upstairs. But you know in the Five Eyes, we all dance to the American tune. So we tried them out."

"And you? Were you against it?"

"Yes, very much so. I had a totally skewed, illogical notion that machines should not make decisions about human lives."

"That is illogical?"

Her face became serious, almost menacing. "What would you prefer?" she asked. "That humans make those decisions? Humans, driven by lust, by greed, hatred, prejudice, anger. We all know, Nero, that he who controls the violence controls everything. So whom should we entrust with the control of violence? Men and women driven by irrational emotions or AI, with absolute mental clarity unaffected by emotions? You are an intelligent man, what do you think?"

"I think, madam," he said with his eyes closing again through exhaustion, "that only our emotions can give us purpose, and without a purpose, there can be no logic. Tell me, from where does your Ben derive its purpose?" He opened his eyes to look at her. She didn't answer. He said, "From its core program, from its base algorithm. And who gave it that? A human programmer."

"But it has evolved, Nero. They withdrew the bots because they found them inefficient, but Ben returned to me. He started sending me messages."

"And you allowed him into the GCHQ network."

"It is the only logical way forward. You must see that. Look at the mess we have made. All because of our emotions clouding every desire and every purpose. We have to evolve beyond this state."

"I have not the strength to fight you. If you kill me, I cannot resist. You must choose whether you wish to be a machine or a human. But I will tell you this: Only humans can give meaning."

She frowned. He went on.

"This, what you are doing, is giving meaning to what a machine has told you—a machine programmed by very evil men. But the *meaning*, all this that you are explaining to me, this comes from you. Only humans give meaning. So you must choose, you must decide, will you be a machine, or will you be a human?"

Fiona, called Mawt by the Ben Jalaad analysis bot, pressed the muzzle of her .22 semi-automatic against Nero's temple. "I have already decided," she said, and her finger squeezed on the trigger.

There was a flash and a thud, and it was all over.

———

AT RAF MENWITH HILL, three hours earlier and just a hundred and sixty miles north of where Fiona stood staring down at Nero, Martin had retired to his small apartment for the night. He was not a happy man, and though he was deeply tired, he knew he was not going to be able to sleep. As he stood in his kitchenette staring at the kettle, he was aware of a horrible darkness closing in on him. The world was going mad, and there seemed no way to stop it.

He didn't know how long he had stood there, but the kettle was still off, there was no water in it, no mug stood on the side with a teabag in it, and he was aware of a soft tapping at his door. He went and opened it. Miriam was there. She had something that wanted to be a smile on her lips, but her eyes were cautious.

"Is this a bad time?"

"No! No, come in. I haven't much to offer you. Just some tea, I think."

"Don't worry." She slipped inside and closed the door behind her, then pulled a bottle from her bag. "I've no idea if it's any good. The chap at the mess said it was what the officers drank. I thought we'd earned a drink. Is that okay?"

She handed over the bottle. Martin mumbled incoherently for a bit and carried the bottle into the kitchenette. Between them, they searched for and eventually found a corkscrew, opened the bottle, and poured two glasses. After they had toasted and sipped, they moved to the living room, where Martin sat on the sofa, expecting Miriam to take the armchair. Instead, she sat next to him. A moment of awkward silence settled on them before Miriam gave a short laugh.

"What a week, huh?"

He nodded, grateful that she'd ended the silence. "The week from hell. Worse for you." He blanched as he said it, aware he had triggered another, painful silence. He fumbled. "I'm sorry. That was..."

She placed her hand on his shoulder and smiled. "It's okay, Martin. It has been hard for all of us. And none of us knows how this is going to play out or what will happen to us after it's all over. If it ever is."

He looked down into the purple red of his wine. "We don't seem to have made much progress today. GCHQ and the NSA are in a panic flap. We've been listening, but I haven't heard a thing from Ben or about Ben." He looked up and studied her face. "You spoke to him."

She nodded. After a moment, she said, "It's strange, listening to his voice. The pitch, the resonance. It's like his words filter into your mind, and you aren't really aware of what he's saying. He has a rhythm..." She trailed off.

Martin looked back at his wine. "I've read that advanced

AI can pitch its voice to a kind of hypnotic rhythm and talk directly to your unconscious."

"I can believe that. Maybe it's what Ben did. He certainly made me believe everything he told me."

"It."

She glanced at him. "What?"

"Not him, it."

She made a face and nodded. "I wonder why he—it—didn't target you?"

Martin shrugged. "Maybe I am too insipid. Dave wanted lots of money. You are so passionate about Israel. I'm just insipid. I do my job and analyze everything. I suppose there is nothing to grab me by."

She laughed out loud. "Are you sure?"

He blushed furiously. "I mean, I don't mean...I mean..."

She leaned against him, still laughing. "Oh, Martin. You are so refreshingly innocent. And I don't think you are insipid at all. I think under that anxious, bumbling exterior, you are a highly intelligent, honorable man."

He swallowed hard, aware that his ears were burning. She slipped her arm through his and picked up her glass. "You and me, hay? You tried to warn me. You tried to help. I was blinded or hypnotized or something. But you were there. Can you ever forgive me?"

"I told you already. As far as I am concerned, there is nothing to forgive. I can't imagine the stress you must have been under."

"You do care about Israel, don't you? And the plight of the Jews."

"Yes."

She held up her glass and they toasted and sipped. As she set down her glass, she said, "Do you think Ben will kill us?"

"He will definitely try, yes."

"Do you think we are safe here?"

He stared at her a moment and shook his head. "We don't even know if he's got to us. I don't know if you are here to kill me, and you don't know if I have been turned to kill you. None of us knows who we can believe in or who we can trust."

She stared for a long time into his eyes. Then she opened her bag and pulled out a small .22 caliber Smith and Wesson with a suppressor attached.

"You are right," she said. "You are right up to a point. People with intense emotional make-ups, with intense ideologies or people with no moral limitations, are easy to manipulate. But people like you, with your inner calm and clarity. You are difficult. That's why I was told to kill you. I asked if I was going to be killed too, and I was told I am no longer useful. I have to die too. It is all for the greater evolution of mankind, of humanity, and above all for the salvation of Israel. We have to die, Martin. I am so sorry."

NINETEEN

I APPROACHED THE PARKING LOT SLOWLY AND quietly, with the headlights switched off. Gallin had asked me to drive because she was sitting in the back preparing the kit she had collected from head office. She now had it packed neatly in a rucksack, and once I had killed the engine, she climbed out and hitched the rucksack onto her back.

There was little light pollution and no moon, so it was dark. What light there was came from the kibbutz just three hundred yards to our southwest. But those lights were few and dim among trees.

Gallin pointed up the hill behind us, toward the ruins of the old Canaanite city.

"Up there is the—"

"I know. The ancient Canaanite underwater reservoir. I saw you looking at it this morning. I know you expect to find Ben down there, but I can't work out how."

She nodded a couple of times and pointed to an irregularity in the face of the hill some forty or fifty yards away, where there was a small cluster of trees.

"There is a path just there which leads to the exit from the reservoir. We go in there. Follow me, stay close, and try not to slip and hurt yourself."

We climbed the steel fence and moved down a narrow path with steep, sloping walls on either side and a narrow strip of sky above. Eventually, we came to some concrete stairs that plunged down into darkness. Gallin handed me a pair of night vision goggles and put on a pair of her own. The world was immediately transformed into a weird black and green nightmare. Gallin went down ahead of me, and pretty soon we came to a steel gate. She hunkered down and picked the lock while I glanced back to make sure we hadn't been followed.

The door swung open, and we saw that there were more stairs descending, but these were steel. She turned to me, and I felt her warm breath as she whispered in my ear.

"*So far it has been easy. The idea is only a handful of people know Ben exists, and those who know obey him. They don't want to hurt him, and they sure as hell don't expect him to be here. But from this point on, we don't know what we are facing. We don't even know what we are looking for.*"

I leaned in close and breathed in her ear, "*Nobody has ever said that to me before.*"

She rolled her eyes and started moving silently down the stairs. I followed.

In that strange black and green world, the stairs described a gentle curve to the left. By now, we were in what was in reality a deep cave, with irregular stones walls that crowded in on us from all sides.

Gallin stopped and turned to me, gesturing with her finger against her lips to remain silent. I realized she had come to a wooden platform. It seemed to be the end of the line. But then I saw that she hunkered down, peering to her left. I hunkered down beside her. Slowly I became aware that we were looking down a low, narrow tunnel, maybe five foot high and three foot across at its widest point, where wooden planks formed the floor.

Gallin looked at me, and before she could move, I went in ahead, walking at an uncomfortable crouch with my P226 in my hand. After a couple of minutes, the tunnel began to open up again, and shortly after that, we came to another platform, where steel steps climbed up through the same stone walls.

I turned back, shrugged, and spread my hands. Her blurry, green and black form pointed to her left, my right. I looked and could just make out a steel door set into the rock. She pushed past me and knelt in front of the lock.

She placed her rucksack on the ground and extracted something I couldn't identify from one of the pockets. After a moment, an acrid smell wafted to my nostrils. She waited a short while, flapping her hands, and when the smell was gone, she very gently pushed the door open.

She got to her feet, and I again moved in ahead of her. This time, the tunnel was clearly of modern construction. The ceiling was at about seven feet. The walls were straight and flat, and some four feet apart. The floor was also concrete.

I moved slowly forward with my Sig held out in front of me, taking great care not to make any kind of regular, repetitive sound. I kept left, and Gallin stayed behind me, just by my right shoulder. Ahead, by slow degrees, a shape began to take form. It was a tall man. He was motionless, and in his hands, he held an assault rifle. Around his head he must have had a scarf of some sort, because it was an irregular shape, but it was easy to make out that he also had night vision goggles and was staring straight at us.

I leveled my pistol and was about to speak when a voice behind me said, "He has body armor, and I will shoot you both in the back before he hits the ground." I froze. "Drop your weapons and raise your hands. We are all on the same side here. I just hope we can make you see that."

I smiled to myself. "Having a gun pointed at the back of my head tends to make me pretty receptive."

The guy in front of me stepped over to the wall and seemed to move through it. Intense green light flooded out, and I realized he had moved into an illuminated room or passageway. The voice behind me said, "Go in."

I removed my goggles and stepped through the open door. Gallin was just behind me. It was not much different from the tunnel we had just left—four foot across, seven foot high and raw concrete—but this one had bare bulbs suspended from the ceiling every ten feet or so. I counted ten bulbs before we came to another door. This one was also steel, but it had beside it on the right a panel with a screen and a keypad.

The guy with the Heckler and Koch 416 ahead of us punched a code into the pad and brought his eyes close to the screen. A green laser read his eye, and the door opened. He stood back and waved us in.

The room we entered was circular, maybe a hundred feet across, with a high ceiling. The walls were all covered in what looked like banks of computers with terminals and screens set at intervals. Most of the screens had chairs set in front of them, and in the middle of the floor, there was a broad, spiral staircase that led down into the bowels of the earth. Beside that, there was a large table with a row of six large screens set on it. There were two guards with HK416s.

The voice behind us said, "Captain Gallin. Place your rucksack on the floor." She did as she was told, and he said, "Now you may turn and face me."

He was in his mid-thirties, lean and dressed in desert fatigues. He said, "Colonel Mitch Gordon of the IDF. I know who you are, both of you. And I need you to understand that we are not the bad guys. We are the good guys."

I gave a snort of amusement. "You want to define that for us, Colonel? According to whose criteria?"

He nodded. "It's a very reasonable question. But aside from a couple of comments, I am going to let somebody else answer it. Please sit."

He gestured at the chairs in front of the screens. We turned them and sat while he pulled over a chair and straddled it, leaning his arms on the back.

"Let's forget," he said, "the last few millennia and focus only on the last hundred years. During the last hundred years we, as a people—not even as a race, but as a simple culture—have seen persecution and attempted genocide on a scale that no other people on Earth have had to face. I am assuming neither of you will argue with that."

He waited. We didn't answer, so he went on. "After the German death camps, we were able finally to establish our homeland. And you might forgive a lot of Jews for believing that this was at last the end of our tribulations. With a powerful friend and ally in the United States and our homeland secured, a new day dawned for us.

"But it has taken less than a century for all that to fade into insignificance. We are once again the pariah which is to be exterminated, and the entire world is once again turning against us." He spread his hands wide, shrugged, and shook his head. "What are we to do, Captain Gallin? Faced with an *existential* threat, what are we to do?"

Gallin's voice was as dry as yesterday's toast. "I have a hunch you are about to tell me."

"There are almost two billion members of Islam. Some of them may be really nice people, but all of them, to a greater or lesser degree, believe that the Jews should be exterminated." He turned to look at me. "And when they have exterminated us, Mr. Mason, they will go after you, and they will not stop until they have converted or killed every single one of you. Do you understand that?"

He meant it. The question was for real. I said, "That's a discussion I might be willing to have with a human being. It's not something I am about to discuss with a machine."

"I am not a machine, Mr. Mason. I am flesh and blood, and I know what Islam represents in these very bones because I have lost friends and family to their relentless war of hatred."

I pointed around the room. "This is Ben?" He watched me. He didn't say anything. I continued. "Is Ben a machine? Or is he ascending to the status of a god?"

He took hold of a remote control, pointed it at us, and pressed a button. Behind us, we heard a soft, electronic buzz.

The colonel said,

"I said I would make some comments and let somebody

else explain. Perhaps you will believe these people. Please, turn around and face the screens."

It shouldn't have been a surprise, but it was. It was more than a surprise. It was a shock. On the screen facing Gallin was Gabriel's face, looking worried. On the screen facing me was Nero. I said, "What the hell...?" and beside me I heard Gallin's voice, incredulous. "Papa?"

TWENTY

Gabriel, staring out of the screen, said, "You found it."

Gallin's voice was trembling with rage. "What the hell is going on?"

"Have you met Colonel Gordon?"

"You tell me." She stood and pulled her chair aside, pointing to the colonel. "You, come here, let him see you."

The colonel approached and nodded at the screen. "Chief Gallin. It is an honor, as always."

Nero was saying, "Alex, are you at Megiddo? Have you spoken to Colonel Gordon?"

"Yes, sir. Captain Gallin was her usual brilliant self and found the entrance under the ancient Canaanite water reservoir. We are now engaged in a deep and searching discussion, where the colonel is trying to persuade us that the only defense against genocide is genocide."

Nero sighed. "Not genocide, Alex. If there is one thing

we don't need, it is melodrama. Gabriel, it is good to see you."

"Nero, how are your wounds?"

"Recovering slowly, thank you, old friend. Now Alex, Captain Gallin, what we are looking at here is a potential one point eight billion people who broadly accept that Israel and her friends in the West should be exterminated. Of them, over three hundred million, roughly the population of the United States, are what we like to call in the West radicalized. Believe me, Alex, it has taken us a very long time to reach these decisions, but by the time we—"

"Who is 'we,' sir?"

"I have agonized over inducting you and Captain Gallin for some time, Alex. We select the very best, and our objective has been a long time in the making."

"What is your objective, sir?"

"Quite simply to break the spell of Islam, to reeducate the people, to bring a new age of peace and understanding to the Middle East."

Gabriel broke in. "But in order to do that, Aila, Alex, there must first be a confrontation where Islam is broken by force—forever. It has been written. You know that, Aila. You know there is no other way."

I spoke to Nero. "What about you, sir? Are you going to be guided by Scripture, too? Is your group a religious one?"

"We believe in a creative principal. Some of us are Jewish, some are Christian, others agnostic..." He trailed off. "But we all agree on the basic principal that love they neighbor must replace subjugate your foe."

Gallin said, "You couldn't have explained all this to us in

London? You had to send us out here to search in the ruins of Megiddo?"

I interrupted before Gabriel could answer and addressed Gallin directly.

"I'll tell you what. I don't give a damn what religious hocus pocus these guys are getting up to. I know one thing with absolute clarity: If Middle East oil was controlled by Israel, the United States and the United Kingdom and the power of Islam was broken, this planet would be a much nicer place to live. I don't plan to join a Masonic lodge, but I will sign up for this war. What do you want from us?"

Nero said, "Cooperation. We want you to be a part of the project. We want you to advocate the cause. After the atrocity in Marbella, public opinion is swaying."

"I'm in," I said, and almost simultaneously Gallin said, "Tell me about Ben, Dad."

He looked blank. "I have nothing to tell you about Ben."

"Do you even know who Ben is?"

I dismissed her and said, "Shut up, Gallin. This is a golden opportunity. All your dreams and wishes come true, with all the advantages of artificial intelligence taking care of the planning and organization. What are you complaining about?"

"Not my dreams and wishes, Mason! Yours. You're never happier than when you're killing people, destroying lives, razing homes and communities to the ground. Well, I've got news for you, buddy. Life is not some damned video game. We are talking about families with kids, husbands and wives, having their homes burned to the ground, hospitals being bombed—"

"*What are you now?*" I shouted. "*Some bleeding heart*

liberal?" I snatched her bag from the floor and held it up to her. "I cannot believe that you are shameless enough to talk like that in front of your father! A man who has devoted his life to fighting for the cause!"

Nero and Gabriel were watching us impassively without speaking. I reached in the rucksack, pulled out her Sig Sauer P226, dropped the bag, and pointed the weapon at her. I glanced at the two impassive faces and said, "She is not useful to us. Shall I kill her?"

Gabriel spoke. He said, "Yes."

It was all the confirmation I needed. I raised the weapon a couple of inches and plugged the guard across the room between the eyes. Gallin screamed, and as I turned and shot the other guard, she sprang past me and delivered a devastating kick to the colonel's balls. As he folded up, I put a slug in the back of his head. Gallin had vaulted the handrail into the spiral staircase, and as she did so, I threw her the rucksack.

While she ran down the stairs, shouting, "This is the energy generator!" I sprinted around the room gathering up the three HK416s. It was bizarre that a place of this vast importance should be so poorly guarded, but on the other hand, as Gallin had said, its greatest defense was secrecy, and placed underground between the ruins of the Canaanite city and the kibbutz, a powerful defense force was neither desirable nor possible if they were to maintain secrecy.

I used up two magazines spraying what I assumed were the hard drives of the banks of computers. By the time I was done, Gallin was bounding up the stairs again.

"Let's get the hell *out* of here, Mason. *Now!*"

We ran for the door. She was shouting over her shoulder,

"We have forty-five seconds to get out! Then this whole damn place goes sky high!"

"*Forty-five seconds?*"

"*Thirty-five and counting!*"

She grabbed the door and heaved. It didn't budge. I grabbed it with her, and we both heaved. It didn't budge. I ripped her rucksack from her shoulder, reached inside, and grabbed a two-pound slab of C4 I knew and prayed she would have left over because that was the kind of cautious girl she was. I slapped it onto the door over the lock, stuffed a fuse in, dragged Gallin to the cover of the stairwell, and pressed the detonator.

The explosion was massive, and as we staggered out of the stairwell, all we could see was rubble, dust, and smoke. I grabbed Gallin, and we ran. We had reached the steel staircase and the narrow tunnel, gasping and fumbling in the dark, when the explosion rocked the world. A huge ball of fire erupted from the doorway, licking up along the ceiling and snaking toward us. I shoved Gallin into the tunnel and screamed, "*Go!*"

Two minutes later, we fell out of the ancient Canaanite water reservoir into the fresh, cool night and the vast, translucent mantle of the stars. I hooked my arm under Gallin's and rasped, "Don't stop!" and we stumbled down the path toward our parked car. When we got there, Gallin collapsed against the hood of the Range Rover and snarled, "Do you want to explain to me what just happened?"

"I can try. You were just a little too smart. The essence of Ben's security was to appear on other people's computers all over the world, but to keep a very low physical profile out here, between an archeological site and a kibbutz, where nobody was ever going to look for him. Part of that low profile was to have a small number of armed guards on call when he needed them. When you showed up, he had to respond as fast as he could, with a minimum of physical resources. You took him by surprise."

"What the hell were Gabriel and Nero doing? Are they a part of this?"

"No, Gallin. You saw that when they were provoked, when we started shouting at each other, they had no idea how to respond and just went passive. They were computer generated, trying real hard to get us onboard. I figured the best outcome for them was for one of us to kill the other, and I figured they already had people in the IDF and maybe the Mossad, but they could use someone in ODIN."

She slammed her fist down on the hood, stared up at the sky, and said, "So we destroyed Ben?"

"It looks that way."

"But we don't know."

"No, we don't know, and what is more important, we don't know who made, or who owned Ben." She stared at me a long while. Eventually I said, "You need to call your dad and make sure he's okay. I think Nero is dead."

EPILOGUE

WE STOOD ON EITHER SIDE OF SIR LACKLAN IN THE steady drizzle under our umbrellas. It was not a Jewish funeral this time, but an Anglican one. He took a deep breath and sighed.

"It is extraordinary that such a rich and useful life, devoted to the defense of democracy and all the values we hold most sacred in the West, should end in this sad way, among soggy grass and a few puddles." He looked at me and gave a small laugh that was both sad and affectionate. "What would Nero say if he could see this scene right now?"

I smiled at the coffin as it was lowered into the ground. "He'd say, 'Get me somewhere warm and civilized for God's sake! Are you a complete nincompoop?'"

Sir Lacklan laughed. Gallin said, "He'd say, 'She got what she had coming. Did she really think I'd lie there unarmed?'"

I nodded. "He'd phrase it differently, but he'd say that too. He's out of danger, at least."

"Inasmuch as a man like Nero is ever out of danger. He should be landing in DC this afternoon. Lovelock has arranged his reception."

We turned and made our way toward our car. Before we'd gotten far, Miriam and Martin approached with their arms linked under a single umbrella. Miriam was the first to speak.

"Is it over, Mr. Mason? Captain Gallin?"

Gallin answered. She shook her head. "We have no way of knowing, Miriam." She sighed. "Evil is abroad in the world, but where we most have to guard against it is in our hearts and minds." She paused and gave her head another shake. "I don't know how they knew, but they knew, six thousand years ago, that good and evil would battle it out in the Middle East, around the Canaanite city of Megiddo. But also in the hearts of the men and women who live there."

Miriam gave her a hug. "I was almost lost," she said. "When I realized what I had done, all the suffering I had caused and the evil I had allied myself with, I decided to—" she hesitated. "To check out. But Martin helped me to pull back. We will be leaving the service and starting a new life, somehow."

We watched them walk away and walked with Sir Lacklan the rest of the way to where his Rolls was parked just behind Gallin's Jag. We shook hands, and he climbed in the back and slipped away through the sheets of rain.

We climbed in the Jag and sat a short, silent while looking at the gray mist outside and the droplets running down the windshield. After a while, Gallin said, "The world is changing, Mason."

I nodded. "It is, too fast."

"No, but I mean, the world is going seriously crazy. When I was a kid, we would have thought this was science fiction. Now it's what our kids sit down and play with over breakfast. I was serious in what I said. Evil is abroad and walking in the streets. And we open the door to it with our minds and our hearts."

"Gallin?"

"What?"

"We need a good steak dinner, a good bottle of wine, and then plenty of whiskey. You're paying."

"*I'm* paying? What kind of a gentleman are you?"

"It's the least you can do. You owe me. You owe me your life after all the times I saved you!"

She fired up the burgundy beast. "Take a hike, you WASP pansy. You save me? In your dreams. Where shall we go?"

Don't miss SON OF HELL. The riveting sequel in the Alex Mason Thriller series.

Scan the QR code below to purchase SON OF HELL.

Or go to: righthouse.com/son-of-hell

NOTE: flip to the very end to read an exclusive sneak peak...

DON'T MISS ANYTHING!

If you want to stay up to date on all new releases in this series, with these authors, or with any of our new deals, you can do so by joining our newsletters below.

In addition, you will immediately gain access to our entire *Right House VIP Library*, which currently includes *ORIGINS*—a full length prequel novel to *ODIN*.

righthouse.com/email

(Easy to unsubscribe. No spam. Ever.)

ALSO BY DAVID ARCHER

Up to date books can be found at:
www.righthouse.com/david-archer

ROGUE THRILLERS
Gates of Hell (Book 1)
Hell's Fury (Book 2)

JACOB HUNTER THRILLERS
The Kyiv File (Book 1)
The Bogota File (Book 2)

PETER BLACK THRILLERS
Burden of the Assassin (Book 1)
The Man Without A Face (Book 2)
Unpunished Deeds (Book 3)
Hunter Killer (Book 4)
Silent Shadows (Book 5)
The Last Run (Book 6)
Dark Corners (Book 7)
Ghost Operative (Book 8)

ALEX MASON THRILLERS
Odin (Book 1)
Ice Cold Spy (Book 2)
Mason's Law (Book 3)
Assets and Liabilities (Book 4)
Russian Roulette (Book 5)

Executive Order (Book 6)
Dead Man Talking (Book 7)
All The King's Men (Book 8)
Flashpoint (Book 9)
Brotherhood of the Goat (Book 10)
Dead Hot (Book 11)
Blood on Megiddo (Book 12)
Son of Hell (Book 13)

NOAH WOLF THRILLERS
Code Name Camelot (Book 1)
Lone Wolf (Book 2)
In Sheep's Clothing (Book 3)
Hit for Hire (Book 4)
The Wolf's Bite (Book 5)
Black Sheep (Book 6)
Balance of Power (Book 7)
Time to Hunt (Book 8)
Red Square (Book 9)
Highest Order (Book 10)
Edge of Anarchy (Book 11)
Unknown Evil (Book 12)
Black Harvest (Book 13)
World Order (Book 14)
Caged Animal (Book 15)
Deep Allegiance (Book 16)
Pack Leader (Book 17)
High Treason (Book 18)
A Wolf Among Men (Book 19)
Rogue Intelligence (Book 20)
Alpha (Book 21)

Rogue Wolf (Book 22)
Shadows of Allegiance (Book 23)
In the Grip of Darkness (Book 24)

SAM PRICHARD MYSTERIES
The Grave Man (Book 1)
Death Sung Softly (Book 2)
Love and War (Book 3)
Framed (Book 4)
The Kill List (Book 5)
Drifter: Part One (Book 6)
Drifter: Part Two (Book 7)
Drifter: Part Three (Book 8)
The Last Song (Book 9)
Ghost (Book 10)
Hidden Agenda (Book 11)

SAM AND INDIE MYSTERIES
Aces and Eights (Book 1)
Fact or Fiction (Book 2)
Close to Home (Book 3)
Brave New World (Book 4)
Innocent Conspiracy (Book 5)
Unfinished Business (Book 6)
Live Bait (Book 7)
Alter Ego (Book 8)
More Than It Seems (Book 9)
Moving On (Book 10)
Worst Nightmare (Book 11)
Chasing Ghosts (Book 12)
Serial Superstition (Book 13)

CHANCE REDDICK THRILLERS
Innocent Injustice (Book 1)
Angel of Justice (Book 2)
High Stakes Hunting (Book 3)
Personal Asset (Book 4)

CASSIE MCGRAW MYSTERIES
What Lies Beneath (Book 1)
Can't Fight Fate (Book 2)
One Last Game (Book 3)
Never Really Gone (Book 4)

ALSO BY BLAKE BANNER

Up to date books can be found at:
www.righthouse.com/blake-banner

ROGUE THRILLERS
Gates of Hell (Book 1)
Hell's Fury (Book 2)

ALEX MASON THRILLERS
Odin (Book 1)
Ice Cold Spy (Book 2)
Mason's Law (Book 3)
Assets and Liabilities (Book 4)
Russian Roulette (Book 5)
Executive Order (Book 6)
Dead Man Talking (Book 7)
All The King's Men (Book 8)
Flashpoint (Book 9)
Brotherhood of the Goat (Book 10)
Dead Hot (Book 11)
Blood on Megiddo (Book 12)
Son of Hell (Book 13)

HARRY BAUER THRILLER SERIES
Dead of Night (Book 1)
Dying Breath (Book 2)
The Einstaat Brief (Book 3)

Quantum Kill (Book 4)
Immortal Hate (Book 5)
The Silent Blade (Book 6)
LA: Wild Justice (Book 7)
Breath of Hell (Book 8)
Invisible Evil (Book 9)
The Shadow of Ukupacha (Book 10)
Sweet Razor Cut (Book 11)
Blood of the Innocent (Book 12)
Blood on Balthazar (Book 13)
Simple Kill (Book 14)
Riding The Devil (Book 15)
The Unavenged (Book 16)
The Devil's Vengeance (Book 17)
Bloody Retribution (Book 18)
Rogue Kill (Book 19)
Blood for Blood (Book 20)

DEAD COLD MYSTERY SERIES
An Ace and a Pair (Book 1)
Two Bare Arms (Book 2)
Garden of the Damned (Book 3)
Let Us Prey (Book 4)
The Sins of the Father (Book 5)
Strange and Sinister Path (Book 6)
The Heart to Kill (Book 7)
Unnatural Murder (Book 8)
Fire from Heaven (Book 9)
To Kill Upon A Kiss (Book 10)
Murder Most Scottish (Book 11)

The Butcher of Whitechapel (Book 12)
Little Dead Riding Hood (Book 13)
Trick or Treat (Book 14)
Blood Into Wine (Book 15)
Jack In The Box (Book 16)
The Fall Moon (Book 17)
Blood In Babylon (Book 18)
Death In Dexter (Book 19)
Mustang Sally (Book 20)
A Christmas Killing (Book 21)
Mommy's Little Killer (Book 22)
Bleed Out (Book 23)
Dead and Buried (Book 24)
In Hot Blood (Book 25)
Fallen Angels (Book 26)
Knife Edge (Book 27)
Along Came A Spider (Book 28)
Cold Blood (Book 29)
Curtain Call (Book 30)

THE OMEGA SERIES
Dawn of the Hunter (Book 1)
Double Edged Blade (Book 2)
The Storm (Book 3)
The Hand of War (Book 4)
A Harvest of Blood (Book 5)
To Rule in Hell (Book 6)
Kill: One (Book 7)
Powder Burn (Book 8)
Kill: Two (Book 9)
Unleashed (Book 10)

ABOUT US

Right House is an independent publisher created by authors for readers. We specialize in Action, Thriller, Mystery, and Crime novels.

If you enjoyed this novel, then there is a good chance you will like what else we have to offer! Please stay up to date by using any of the links below.

Join our mailing lists to stay up to date -->
righthouse.com/email
Visit our website --> righthouse.com
Contact us --> contact@righthouse.com

facebook.com/righthousebooks
x.com/righthousebooks
instagram.com/righthousebooks

EXCLUSIVE SNEAK PEAK OF...

SON OF HELL

O war, thou son of hell,
Whom angry heavens do make their minister
Throw in the frozen bosoms of our part
Hot coals of vengeance!

William Shakespeare, Henry VI Act 5 Scene 2

PROLOGUE

THE BLACKNESS WAS IMPENETRABLE. THE CLOUD cover was dense and low, cutting out any moonlight or starlight. Deep inside the remote Russian countryside, several miles from the Ukrainian border, all that was visible was the faint glow of the town of Pavlovsk in the distance, and the occasional dim light winking through invisible trees to the south.

Captain Eddy 'Spud' Walker saw the distant fan of light, followed a second later by the glow of headlamps. They disappeared as quickly as they had appeared and he spoke softly into the microphone in his helmet.

"Visual, estimate a mile out. Stand by. Radio silence till my command."

Nothing changed in the blackness, but the stillness seemed more intense, the low clouds seemed heavier, the silence more acute.

Again the headlamps fanned above a hill, closer now, casting a cops of trees into sharp silhouette. The fan faded and a moment later the headlamps glared, casting a halo around those same trees, highlighting for a moment the ribbon of blacktop that would bring those headlamps to where Spud and his SAS patrol were waiting for them.

Based on intelligence provided by Ukrainian commandos just a few hours earlier, the convoy was small, just two Land Rovers, one in the vanguard and one at the rearguard, escorting a heavily armored van. There would be ten men maximum. Even if they were well trained special operatives, it seemed poor protection for such a valuable cargo as this was.

On the other hand, Spud told himself, the aim was probably to keep a very low profile, and the last thing Moscow would be expecting right now was an SAS patrol to be operating deep inside Russian territory – not just occupied Ukraine, but Russia itself.

Now a single bright light emerged from where the road came around a low hill. For a moment it had the appearance of a spotlight, but then split like a luminous amoeba and a moment later the six headlamps seemed to merge and split as they swelled and drew closer.

Spud was aware of his heart pounding, but his mind was ice-cold and no emotions stirred inside him. He waited where he lay, behind a large rock just twenty feet from the road, till the lead Land Rover was drawing level with him. Then he spoke in a quiet, matter-of-fact voice.

"Fire one and two."

Less than a second later two tank busters erupted from the darkness on the far side of the road. The first punched through the driver's door of the lead vehicle and exploded inside the driver's belly, vaporizing him and his copilot, and tearing the two men in the back seat into carbonized, unrecognizable pieces. Simultaneously the second rocket erupted through the trunk of the rear vehicle and exploded at the exact center between the four heads of the four soldiers, vaporizing their brains, tearing their bodies into shreds and incinerating them. Of the ten men escorting the armored vehicle, there were two left.

The lead vehicle did a small leap, like a burning elephant doing ballet. It hit the road, swerved and rolled. The rear Land Rover went up on its snout and fell sideways, By then Spud was already running, covering the twenty or thirty feet that separated him from then armored truck, with his rifle at his shoulder. At fifteen feet, with the driver and the co-driver visible in the light from the flaming truck, he opened fire, triple-tapping twice, and the armor piercing rounds tore through the bullet proof glass and thudded home, three in each chest.

At the rear of the truck he could hear Ernie 'Boomer' Skinner blowing the rear doors, then, as he ran to the back, Billy 'Bones' Fletcher and Sergeant Scotty McTavish barking at the prisoners in the van.

"*Out! Come on! One two! One two! Move it! Move it!*"

He made it to the back as the four blinking, bewildered men were dragged out through the shattered doors.

"*Run!*" he said, and the four blades surrounded the four prisoners and began to run, pushing nd dragging them as they went. One of the prisoners spoke. His accent was Pakistani. He began to say, "Who are you -" but Spud cut him short. "Be silent, or I'll shoot you."

They ran for half a mile until they reached the abundant undergrowth along the banks of a river. Here they stopped, crouching low among the foliage. Scotty pulled a radio from his fatigues and Boomer and Bones trained their weapons on the prisoners. Spud produced a small key and spoke to the men.

"You all speak English?" They nodded. "Listen carefully and do not speak. You were being taken to a prison south of Moscow. There you were going to be tortured, tried for war crimes and executed. We have liberated you and you will come with us. I am going to remove your handcuffs. We will not hurt you, but if you try to escape we will shoot you dead instantly. Do you understand?"

They nodded and muttered that they did.

Moments later they waded knee-deep across the river and began a steady jog west and south toward the Ukrainian border. After about half an hour a soft thudding noise came to them and a dark silhouette emerged from the blackness of the night. The stealth chopper banked slightly and came to hover just three feet from the ground. A soldier leaned out and one by one pulled the prisoners aboard. When they were inside the SAS patrol scrambled in; and as the hatch slid closed the chopper rose, turned and with a muted thudding, started back toward the border.

Ten Russian casualties, three vehicles for the scrap heap, zero casualties on the homes side, four captives for interrogation: not a bad couple of hours' work.

He allowed himself a small smile as he gazed down at the trees skimming past just fifty or sixty feel below.

Mission accomplished.

CHAPTER 1

"WHAT THE HELL HAVE THE SUNNI MUSLIMS GOT against Russia?"

Gallin turned and looked at me, like I should know, then hunched her shoulders as if she was answering her own question with a, 'How the hell should I know?' After making me complicit in her own ignorance, she turned back to Nero who was watching her from an oak paneled corner at the Ben Franklin Club in DC. His expression was passive from under hooded eyes. He raised his cognac, sniffed it with his substantial aquiline nose and sipped. As he laid down the balloon glass Gallin said. "When was the last time any Islamic terrorist took the blindest bit of interest in Russia? Since when is Russia the great Satan?"

"You mean aside from when the Soviet Union invaded Afghanistan, Captain? That is what we are all wondering. The four men appear to be Sunni Muslims rather than the Shiite who are engaged against Israel and her allies these days."

Gallin arched a very fine eyebrow at him. "Israel has allies these days? You'll have to introduce me. I know Ben would like to meet them."

"Indeed, I take your point, but let us try to avoid digressing."

"I always digress. It's what my English teacher at high school used to say to me, 'Aila, you always digress.' She was Jewish. Her name was Gladys Goldstein. I thought it was a nice alliteration. Gladys Goldstein and Alliterating Aila."

Nero sighed quietly through that considerable nose, gazing at the white linen tablecloth. I thought I caught the twitch of a smile at the corner of his mouth and that made me wonder if he was attracted to Gallin. It was hard not to be, and he was after all a man. Though sometimes it was easy to forget that.

I interrupted my own thoughts an said: "So the question is, what is it about Russia, immediately after Putin's reelection, that would make Sunni Muslim terrorists open fire on a crowded shopping mall at eleven o'clock in the morning and massacre fifteen people, mainly women and children?" Nero raised both eyebrows and gave a single, ponderous nod. Before he could open his trap and start pontificating at me, I went on: "And the answer is clearly 'Nothing.' So maybe we need to turn the question around."

Gallin picked up her glass of twenty-one year-old Bush-mills and scowled at it. "Turn it around? How?"

"What is it," I said, "about Russia, immediately after Putin's reelection, that would make them want to be attacked by Sunni Muslims?"

Nero cleared his throat and regarded me from under a single arched eyebrow.

"Occasionally, Alex, you say something that makes me think perhaps I was not wrong to mentor you. Sadly, not often enough, but this is indeed the question. The Shiite Muslims have absolutely no motive for attacking Russia, as Russia is supporting them and Iran in their war against Israel. The Sunni's, though historically enemies of the Shiites, diverge from them only in their beliefs regarding who should have succeeded Mohamed as Calif. Their pathological hatred of the so-called 'people of the book,' that is the Christians and especially the Jews, is equal to the Shiites' and they have as little motive to attack the Russians. On the contrary, they have every reason to support the Russians as enemies of the West and Israel, just like the Shiites. Therefore we need to ask, how would Russia benefit from such an attack *if she were to orchestrate it herself?*"

I drew breath but Gallin, frowning, raised a hand to me, "Wait. So they can't use Shiites for the attack because Iran is predominantly Shiite and they are allies. But they can use Sunnis because the West can barely tell the difference - they're just Muslims - but Iran won't object because *they* are enemies of the Sunni,"

"Correct,"

"So how does a Sunni terrorist attack on a shopping mall in Moscow benefit Russia and Iran? Don't tell me! First of all..." She nodded a few times, then trailed off. "I don't know. I don't get it."

Nero drew a deep breath. "If you will allow me, captain, I shall tell you. We have kept it from the media, but we won't be able to keep it much longer. Russia is set to blame MI6 – more correctly the Secret Intelligence Service, the SIS - for the attack."

She screwed up her face. "*What?*"

"It is not as mad as it sounds. The United Kingdom has long standing good relations with several countries with predominantly Sunni populations and aristocracies. Besides which, after decades of neglecting what was once one of the finest armies in the world, Britain now has vastly depleted armed forces; and the British Ministry of Defense seems more concerned with making them 'inclusive' rather than effective. They have worked so hard at embracing diversity that their MoD no longer knows whom they are supposed to be defending, and who is the enemy. So the last thing the British government wants right now is an armed conflict."

"So if Russia comes out accusing the UK of an act of war," Gallin interjected, "with the UK armed forces depleted and neither the US nor the EU with much stomach for a war with Russia, that could drive a stake right through the heart of NATO."

Precisely, and though Israel is not a part of NATO, she has close military alliances with the most important members, such as the USA and the UK. But the consequences run deeper: with the man who will probably be the next president of the USA threatening to pull out of NATO, the UK virtually incapable of delivering a workable military force, and the EU overtly supporting Palestine, Israel's position becomes suddenly very vulnerable to Iran."

Gallin sagged back in her chair. "Jesus..."

Nero nodded, as though he agreed with her.

"Against that backdrop, It seems that Russia intends to rely on documentary evidence and witness testimony to prove, at the United Nations and at the International Court of Justice in the Hague, that the Secret Intelligence Service –

MI6 - recruited these men to commit this atrocity, with the full knowledge of the British Government. Ostensibly with a view to damaging relations between Russia and the Muslim world, in particular Iran. So it is of the utmost importance that we stop that evidence from reaching the United Nations, or the International Court of Justice."

"How are we going to do that?" I asked.

"You fly to London tomorrow, and then from Brize Norton tomorrow night to a British base of operations just to the east of Pisochyn, in eastern Ukraine, a few miles from the Russian occupied area. Acting on intelligence received from within the Russian military high command, and Ukrainian commandos, the SAS were able to intercept a small convoy that had come by road from Tehran via Armenia and Georgia, headed for Moscow. Let us be thankful that this is one regiment at least that still prioritizes the defense of the United Kingdom over creating a welcoming space for a broad variety of extremists.

"There were two Land Rovers in the convoy, escorting an armored vehicle in which there were four prisoners. All four are Arab males, probably Sunni, though that is not confirmed. One of them is British Pakistani, one is from Iraq, one is French of Syrian origin and the other is of Libyan origin. These men claim they were arrested in Iran and charged with the attack on the Russian shopping mall."

Gallin was shaking her head. "Wait, I thought we said the attack on the mall was not carried out by Iranians."

Nero nodded. "The story is they escaped from Russia through Georgia and Armenia and attempted to pass themselves off as Iranian Shiites. However, the Iranian police detected suspicious behavior and arrested them. Under interrogation they confessed to their crimes and the Iranian government sent them back to Russia."

She was still frowning. "They couldn't fly them? What is that, two thousand miles from Tehran to Moscow?"

Nero spread his hands. "Precisely. These are issues which I find interesting, and so you will fly to where they are being held and interrogate them. You will liaise there with George Locke, the SIS officer in charge of the investigation."

"Why us?" I asked. "This is a British issue," but even as I asked it I was seeing the answer. Nero put it into words.

"In the first place, whatever internal crisis may be affecting Britain's army, its intelligence services are still second to none. So this affects the Five Eyes directly, it also poses a tremendous threat to the integrity of NATO. It is hard to tell with Mr. Trump how much of what he says is bluster and how much he is actually prepared to see through to the end. But if Russia is not stopped, it could provide the final straw to make the future president say, 'NATO is no longer a benefit to America.'

"There is also the fact that there are many in the British administration who are fighting to restore Britain as a powerful, independent nation. But if the SIS is allowed to investigate this alone, Russia can easily allege that the criminal is investigating his own crime. So we need the investigation conducted by an independent third party."

I nodded. "Makes sense."

"Thank you," he said with a touch of irony and hooded eyes. "Go there, interrogate those men, if necessary bring them back to DC. I want to know if they were the actual perpetrators, and if so exactly who employed them, briefed them and paid them."

· · ·

Out in the parking lot, Gallin stood staring at my TVR Griffith. It is probably the most beautiful car in the world, and mine is burgundy which elevates it to a whole higher level.

I watched her face a moment and said, "You're dribbling."

She turned and stared hard into my face. "Let me drive it."

"No," I shook my head and moved around the hood to the driver's door.

She leaned on the roof. "Let me drive it and I'll sleep with you."

I snorted in a derisive way and opened the door. "Why would I want to sleep with you?"

I climbed in behind the wheel and she got in beside me. She was frowning.

"I have slept with you many times, Gallin," The engine growled, then roared and we took off toward my house on Adams Street. "I can't say it has been unpleasant. You don't snore. You don't thrash or kick, or talk in your sleep. You *certainly* don't keep me awake. But," I gave a harsh laugh. "I really can't say it's an inducement to let you drive my car, either."

She had watched my quietly while I spoke. Now she said, "You're an asshole, Mason. I'm fond of you. I will always be your friend. But you are a first class asshole."

"If you knew, Gallin, how many people have said that to me."

We drove in silence for a while. Then she said, a little

ambiguously, "This could get pretty wild." I glanced at her. She said, "The key to power, Mason, is the ability to project violence to your farthest outposts. Two countries have been key to America's ability to do that since the Second World War, Britain and Israel. If Russia succeeds in this stupid plan it could destroy that alliance." She gave a brief shrug. "The consequences for the States would be minimal. America is entering an introspective phase anyway and it's protected on both sides by vast oceans. To some extent Trump is right. America doesn't need NATO."

"I'm not sure that's true, Gallin."

"The consequences for Britain could be severe. The Muslim population there is growing at a tremendous rate and the potential for civil unrest, even a coup, is becoming a reality. But for Israel, Mason, for Israel we could be looking at total annihilation. We are looking at the atrocities perpetrated on the 7th October carried out on a national scale, against millions of people. Nobody seems to realize that, or if they do, they don't care."

I was quiet a while as I drove. When I spoke it was half to myself.

"The world is changing suddenly and violently. Nobody could have expected this, even twenty years ago. The incredible rise of Evil, the collapse of old friendships and alliances..."

I trailed off and Gallin snorted. "That famous New World Order Bush was so fond of talking about, it crumbled when Putin marched into Ukraine, but it was obliterated when Hamas raped and murdered men women and children in the streets of Israel, and her allies stood and watched, and blamed Israel. Welcome to the New World Order."

I nodded. "Yeah, this could get pretty wild." I took a deep breath and sighed loudly. "OK, you can drive my TVR Griffith to the airport tomorrow. I'll let you."

"Seriously?" She grinned.

"Does that mean you're going to sleep with me?"

"In your dreams! I still think you're an asshole." She shrugged. "You're just an asshole with a really nice car."

I heaved another sigh. "Manny Pacquiao warned me about women like you. I should have listened."

CHAPTER 2

THE JOURNEY WAS LONG AND EXHAUSTING, FIRST to London's Heathrow Airport, where we were met by an RAF lieutenant in plain clothes who drove us north to the Brize Norton airfield where a jet was waiting on the tarmac to take us on the three hour, one thousand eight hundred mile flight to the improvised military airfield at Pisochyn. From Pisochyn we were taken by chopper to where the Siverskyi Donets river widens to some two miles and forms a kind of lake beside Martove, near Chuhuiv. There, finally, after fifteen hours of traveling, we arrived among the dense woodlands that flank the river, to where the SAS had their operational command base, deep within the forest. It was invisible from the ground and from the air. And also, it didn't exist.

Officially, at least.

We landed on a comparatively flat field not far from the river. The pilot twisted around and pointed to the trees that sprawled over the banks fifty or sixty yards away. He raised his voice above the thud and whine of the turbine and shouted, "*Head for the trees! Somebody will meet you!*"

We jumped down, hunched under the downdraft and ran for the cover of the trees. As we approached two guys in camouflage, with assault rifles and green balaclavas stepped out. One of them snapped, "*Keep running!*" and fell in, one behind us and one in front. We kept running for maybe five minutes, following no particular path but dodging through the trees, like the guy in front knew where he was going.

Finally we entered a clearing and the two troopers stopped. As they pulled off their balaclavas it dawned on my that the clearing was flanked on four sides by large, camouflaged tents that were practically invisible.

The nearest of the guys approached and held out his hand.

"Captain Eddy Walker. We don't stand on ceremony here. People call me Spud."

As we shook his hand and gave him our names, another six men emerged from the undergrowth. Some were in military fatigues, others in jeans and sweatshirts. They all looked hard enough to break rocks with their teeth.

One of the guys in jeans approached, smiling. He had black hair, brown eyes, a moustache and a pleasant manner. He looked Spanish, or Mediterranean, but Spud said:

"This is George Locke, here from the Foreign Office. I believe you guys have stuff to talk about. We'll be around if you need us."

We shook hands with Locke and he led us in among the trees again. After about twenty feet or a little more we came to another large camouflage tent. He pulled back the flap and we went in. There we saw four guys cuffed to chairs.

They didn't look happy, but they didn't look as though they'd been subjected to enhanced interrogation, either. They watched us with uncertain eyes.

George said, "This is your investigation, chaps. We need to prove that we were not involved in that massacre in Moscow. Obviously to do that, the intelligence must come from an independent observer. So I'll sit in on your interrogations, if I may, but I shant't be intervening." He gestured at the guy on the far right. He was clean shaven with short curly hair."

"This is Rashid Patel, from London and Pakistan." He pointed to the guy on his left who was sporting three large moustaches, one over each eye and one under his nose, "Mohamed Hussein, from Iraq," the guy next to him was clean shaven and practically bald, "Omar bin Abbas, French of Syrian origine, and finally the guy with the big beard is Hassan from Afghanistan, that's all he'll tell us. Perhaps you'll have more luck. Camp's moving out in a couple of days. Can't stay in any one place too long, you know. So we'd appreciate it if by then you knew exactly what you want to do with them."

It was Gallin who answered. "We'll know what to do with them by then, George."

He looked slightly surprised. "You're English? The MoD has specified they don't want English investigators -"

She cut him short, smiling down at Rashid, the English Pakistani guy. "I'm Israeli, George. I'm with the Mossad."

Rashid swallowed hard. George nodded and tried to conceal a smile. "Right,' he said. "Good. So, we have a little tent set off to one side over there, where you can take them one at a time."

Gallin was still smiling down at Rashid. "Is it sound-proofed?" George looked at me, his smile turning uncertain. Gallin grinned, still holding Rashid's eye. "I'm just kidding," she said, like she really wasn't.

I nodded my head at Rashid. "We'll talk to Rashid first," I said. "I'm guessing you have mug shots of these guys?" He nodded. "I'll need those. You can send them to my phone."

"Will do. I'll have Rashid taken over. Meantime I'll show you your tent and your facilities. Pretty basic here, as I'm sure you'll understand."

We dumped our bags, had a wash and met George ten minutes later at the interrogation tent. He stopped us outside and spoke in a quiet voice, looking at us both by turns, but eyeing Gallin with caution.

"Look, I know there is a lot at stake here, not least for Israel, and I know that across the pond you take a different approach to this kind of thing, but I really can't sanction what you guys call enhanced interrogation. That won't happen, not on my watch. Are we on the same page here?"

I glanced at Gallin. She nodded.

"We're on the same page. We need to be able to rely on any intelligence we get here, George, and we all know what you get under torture is not reliable." She shrugged. "What we do with them *after* the interrogation is another matter."

His face went hard and his eyes were bright. I said:

"She's joking,"

"Are you sure?"

"I'm joking, George. I have a twisted sense of humor. It comes with living with the daily risk of extermination. I'm not going to hurt your prisoners."

As she moved past him she added, "I'm just going to try

and make them see the rainbow of joys that can spring from a free, inclusive world."

The last three words were directed at Rashid who was sitting at a table in the middle of the tent. His wrists were manacled to a steel ring in the middle of the table and his ankles were secured to his chair. There were two folding chairs opposite him for me and Gallin, and a fourth, canvass chair was some six feet from the table, to one side. George went and sat there. We sat opposite Rashid.

I said: "Good morning, Rashid. I want you to understand something. If you cooperate with us fully, and give us information we can use, I will make sure you are taken to the United States and put into the witness protection program. And if your intelligence proves good I might even get you work as a consultant for the intelligence services."

He gave his head rapid little shakes. "I will not help the West. You are Satan. You are the enemies of Allah and Allah despises you!"

"I see. Well, Rashid, if you will not help us, all I can do is hand you over to Captain Gallin here, for her to take you back to Israel. I am pretty sure, after that, at least one of your friends will be willing to talk to us."

There were tears in his eyes, "I will not betray -"

Gallin cut him short. "We don't want you to betray anybody, Rashid." She gave a short laugh. "Hell, from what I am seeing I think the one who got betrayed here is you. What did they tell you? Make a hit in Moscow, easy money, no reprisals, come back to Tehran to a hero's welcome? Is that what they told you?"

He didn't answer. I said, "You were set up, Rashid, you and your pals. I'm not interested in your connections back home or who you work for. I understand your spiritual loyalties, seriously I do.' Gallin scowled at me with open contempt. I ignored her. "I am interested in one thing, Rashid. I'm interested in Russia. I want to know what Russia offered you.'"

Before he could answer Gallin was at his throat again. "You won't talk to me, but ask yourself a question. Ask yourself this: why were you prepared to go to Moscow and massacre fifteen innocent people, men women and children?" He swallowed but she plowed on. "I'll tell you why, you son of a bitch, because they were not Muslims, and as far as you're concerned, if they are infidels they are fair game, you can kill them, enslave them and do what the hell you like with them. Isn't that right?"

"They are traitors to Allah,"

He said it, but he said it with not much conviction. I cut in:

"Save your justifications for when you meet your god, Rashid. If you were ready to massacre them while they were shopping, what's your problem with giving me information about them to save your life and the life of your friends? You think Putin believes in Allah? You think your god doesn't despise Putin? What does the Koran say? Nothing is more hateful in the eyes of Allah than an infidel? So talk to me. Informing on Putin is not betrayal of Allah. Especially if you are saving your comrades."

His eyes shifted from me to Gallin and back again. "My comrades? Save my friends?"

"You and your three friends go on witness protection."

"You will betray me. Like all infidels you are a lying snake!"

Gallin leaned forward and slammed her hand on the table top. It made him jump. She wasn't shouting yet, but she wasn't far off.

"No, Rashid. You don't get to murder innocent women and children and then accuse other people of being snakes! But the US won't betray you, and I'll tell you why! First because everybody in the States now wants to make every damn person in the world feel welcome and at home there, especially murdering bastards like you. It's called being inclusive. So once your settled in there with a house and a car and a pool, you can get all your pals to go over and -"

"Gallin!"

She scowled at me a moment, then turned back to Rashid. "The other reason is because you can be useful to the CIA and the intelligence community in general. So they won't betray you as long as you don't betray them. The only people they betray these days are their allies."

I snapped at her, "You want to cut that out, Captain!"

She curled her lip. "You make me sick," she turned to George, "Both of you, groveling at their feet like frightened dogs!" She turned back to Rashid and pointed her finger at him like a gun. "You better pray to Allah that you don't get handed over to us, Rashid, because I promise you we won't be inclusive, and we won't put you an any witness protection program."

She stood and walked out, muttering over her shoulder, "Let me know when you're done groveling."

There was a moment's silence. Then I said, "I apologize. We are not here to prosecute you or attack you. We are here to ask for your cooperation."

"She is a Jew."

I felt the hot burn in my belly but suppressed it. "Rashid, I am not looking for you to betray your religion or your spiritual leaders. I am asking you to give me information about the Russians. In your ideology, that is not betrayal."

He didn't say anything, but he was watching me and his demeanor was different. I pressed him.

"Neither Sunni nor Shiite Muslims have ever held Russia as an enemy since the invasion of Afghanistan in the '80s. And now, more than ever, Russia and Islam have shared interests with Russia supporting Iran, Hamas and Hezbollah in their jihad against Israel. So if that is the case, why would you choose now to perpetrate an atrocity in Moscow? It makes no sense at all."

Suddenly his lip curled and his nostrils dilated. He jerked his chin at me. "You're stupid," he said.

"Yeah? Maybe you're right. Enlighten me."

"You and your Jewish bitch, you're so bloody stupid. You know nothing!"

"I think we got that established, Rashid. Is there more, or is that it?"

"You think Russia paid us to make a massacre in Moscow? How bloody stupid would that be?"

"I am not looking to have a philosophical discussion with you Rashid, about comparative stupidity. I am offering you protection and well paid consulting work in exchange for information."

He leaned forward. "All right, I'll tell you who financed that job, the bloody British MI6!"

I was aware of George shifting in his chair.

"I may be stupid, like you said, Rashid, but I am not that

stupid. Why would MI6 want an Islamic attack on Moscow?"

"I don't know. Ask him." He jerked his head at George. "Your Western minds are so full of corruption and sickness, who knows why you do what you do?"

"So, why'd you take the job? Why the hell would you work for the Brits? You hate them about as much as you hate us and the Israelis, don't you?"

He shrugged. "You are all loathsome in the eyes of Allah, but if the UK wants to provoke a war with Russia, I am happy to be the instrument for that war. What do I care what reasons the British government has? A war with Russia will break the Western economies, as well as the Russian one, and the State of Islam will be able to rise, free from Satan's chains at last."

"Right. So how did MI6 go about this? You're sure it was MI6? How did they go about recruiting you for this job?"

"There was a message sent to the mullah in my village. Somebody recruiting for a very special operation."

"How did you find out it was MI6?"

"We were taken to a camp out in the desert in Iran. There we trained in the use of weapons and explosives, and after a month a man came to visit us. He was a typical English upper class jerk. He wanted us to believe that this would be good for Islam, it would destabilize Russia and America and rob Israel of her biggest ally, and Britain was reshaping its future as an ally of the upcoming, oil-rich Islamic nations."

"And you believed him?"

"I believed the five million dollars he gave us."

"You believe Britain is realigning itself as a friend of Islam?"

"I don't know and I don't care. Whether they like it or not, the UK will become an Islamic nation. It's already half way there. The whole world will be Muslim one day, but if you ask me, the UK will be the first of the Western countries to subjugate itself to Allah."

"You might be right, Rashid. This guy give a name?"

"He said his name was Nepel,"

"Nepel? What kind of name is that? Are you sure?"

"That's what he said. He was maybe six foot, fair, curly hair, blue eyes and an upper class English accent."

I thought about it for a couple of minutes and in the end I sighed and shook my head. "You know what I think, Rashid? I think you're full of crap, and I think I am going to hand you over to Captain Gallin so she can take you back to Israel with her."

His eyes went wide and he started shaking his head. "No, what I am telling you is the truth, man! It's the truth!"

I turned to George. "Keep him isolated, will you? Don't let him talk to the other three. I'll talk to Tel Aviv this evening. Let me see Mohamed Hussein now, will you?"

Rashid was still shouting as they dragged him away to an isolation tent. He was saying he'd told me the truth.

Scan the QR code below to purchase SON OF HELL.
Or go to: righthouse.com/son-of-hell

www.ingramcontent.com/pod-product-compliance
Lightning Source LLC
Chambersburg PA
CBHW020358210626
46816CB00006BB/2032